CW00433298

ABRAHAM
SOAR

ABRAHAM SOAR

WILLIAM BLYGHTON

Copyright © William Blyghton, 2018

The right of William Blyghton to be identified as the
author of this work has been asserted by him in accordance
with the Copyright, Designs and Patents Act 1988.

All rights reserved. No part of this publication may be reproduced,
stored in a retrieval system or transmitted in any form or by
any means (electronic, mechanical, photocopying, recording or
otherwise), without the prior written permission of the author.

This is a work of fiction. Names, characters and incidents
are either the product of the author's imagination or
are used fictitiously. Any resemblance to actual events
or persons, living or dead, is entirely coincidental.

Abraham Soar is the second book in The Suffolk Trilogy.

ISBN: 978-1-7294-0440-9

Published by Panacea Books, an imprint of The Write Factor
www.thewritefactor.co.uk

Contents

v

Preface

Abraham Soar is the second part of The Suffolk Trilogy. It began with *The House by the Marsh* and the third part is underway. Based in the coastal region of Suffolk with its rivers, marshes and shingle beaches, the Trilogy has two common themes: loss and love in later life and living in troubled times. In *The House by the Marsh*, William finds himself living in the village of Frampton, close to the marshes. *Abraham Soar* brings us to the very edge of the county, overlooking the North Sea. But who is Abraham and why has he come to live with me?

William Buggler, Suffolk

CHAPTER ONE

I am Abraham Soar. Although that is not strictly true. It cannot be, because I am not entirely of this world. That's obvious isn't it? Here I am, on the page, and so you must see that I am just someone made up by William Blyghton, to let him say things without anyone knowing it's him saying them – which is silly really, since everyone will know it's him. That's what it's like for authors, always pretending to be someone else. So, here I am. On the page. Written down. Abraham Soar.

I have to tell you that although William has written my name, he is not sure who I am. He has imagined me, but he doesn't know why. You see, he is frightened, and he began this story in the hope that it would ease his fear. But now I am here, he doesn't know what to do with me, and that's because he doesn't know what to do with himself. He is stuck.

He has made me in his own image – an old man. Now why choose this? Why couldn't he have made me a young man, an adventurer sailing across oceans and making love to wondrous women on foreign shores – or nearby the shore, since sand is such a problem when making love actually *on* the shore; unless, of course it is pebbled, when it's just very uncomfortable. Well, William couldn't make me a young man because he has forgotten what that feels like. So, here I am, Abraham Soar. An old man – or so it seems.

When I say I am a fiction, I have to tell you that from where I'm standing it seems we are all fictions. You as well as me. The bits we see of each other are what we've made up. Or someone has. Over time. Because of what William has written, what you see is Abraham Soar, elderly and wearing brown lace-up shoes, black corduroy trousers, a white shirt buttoned to the neck, with a scarf and a cardigan. But that's not really me. It's part of the fiction. It's the clothes that William has chosen for someone he has called Abraham Soar. And I'm not sure I would have chosen them. I'm wearing someone else's clothes. I don't mind them. At least they're comfortable, which as we shall see is important to me. They'll do. And William has provided me with a long overcoat, which I like. I wear it all the time. It is blue and of soft wool, and it reaches down to my ankles. And a woollen hat, too. Grey. For the summer he has given me a Panama hat. I like that.

Sorry to go on about this, I know it's difficult, but we must get it right. So, bear with me. Otherwise you will only see what William has written down. The surface. You will have no idea what it is to be me, the me you cannot see behind the me you do see. Of course, you can't see me, not *me*. Only I know me, and even that is difficult. I would like you to know me, but here's a thing: as I have said, William doesn't really know this 'Abraham Soar' whose name he has written down. How could he? Not yet. He may think I am as he is, part of his fearfulness, and in a way I am. But there is more to it than that. Let me try to explain.

At one and the same time, I am both what William writes down and something that he cannot know. He can describe me in the present, but there is part of me that lies beyond the present. I am both here and not here. I am his dæmon. I come from his inner-most being, his soul, but I am both all of him and more than he can be. Can you imagine such a thing? William may have written me as old, but I'm not old. Not in the everyday sense. I'm not young either, or middle-aged. You see, where I have come from there is no age, and so I don't feel any age at all. I am ageless. I am part of who William is, but not limited by that part that has grown old and fearful. I am his inner spirit and the outward expression of his hopes and fears. I am both the one who troubles him and the one who offers him comfort. It may seem to be a contradiction, but that, dear reader, is how it is when you summon up your dæmon. And now William is sitting in his study wondering what to do with me.

Where was I? Yes, here I am, on the page, shaped by William. His elderly man. A man living by himself, as is often the case with elderly people, although I don't quite live by myself. Well, I do in the sense that I am often on my own, but of course, I live with William. I have to. And that's not so bad. William has a comfortable house – and I like comfort, remember that – in the Suffolk seaside town of Aldeburgh. It's back from the sea in a quiet road, almost hidden within a garden that looks west. I like west – endings, the evening, the dusk, the fading light. I don't like south or midday. Too hot, too bright. I also like east and the morning. Beginnings. Renewal. I like that, too. But William's house looks west. The house is all on one level, and its outer walls are roughly plastered and painted an earth yellow under an overhanging pan-tiled roof. The house has large wooden sash windows painted grey, and oak boarded floors some of which have been covered with sea-grass carpeting, which is rough on the soles of bare feet – I often wear no shoes – and some of which has been covered with large antique rugs, which are soft. I have my own bedroom and bathroom, and because William spends most of his time in his study, writing, I have the run of the house. I particularly like the garden room, which has a high-pitched ceiling, two large white sofas and French doors looking into the garden. I often sit in this room, looking out at the garden. West. I like sitting and looking. Do you do that?

As you can imagine – can you imagine this? – I cannot go very far from wherever William is, or at least I cannot go far from where his house is. So, when William goes to London, I stay close to the house, because even when he is not there I feel his presence all around me, holding me to him. That is just how all this works. I am dependent upon him holding me, keeping me in mind, his mind, his imagination. If we are too far apart, or if he forgets about me, I become breathless and begin to fade. I can, however, walk as far as the river and the sea. I walk past the tennis courts, along by the allotments, out over the marshes, along the river wall and then back along the sea front, along Crag Path, returning home up the town steps. That's not too far. No one speaks to me, of course, unless William makes it happen. Otherwise, no one can see me. Although I am used to it, I think you would find it to be the strangest thing. You see, although I have a body, other people can only see it if William writes it down. Then he has to explain my being there, has to invent a story around me, and often he forgets or can't be bothered, so I am left unseen. Some days I sit by myself on the shingle and watch the seabirds swoop and dive, crying out to each other, and perhaps to me. I like that.

But I spend most of my time with William, waiting to be what he writes. He is not always in the mood to write anything at all. In fact, if he's distracted with something else, which is often, I can spend days and weeks just mouldering away in the house. And the worst is when he gets writer's block, because then I'm stuck! Like him. And now there is not even Tinkerbelle to talk to.

I should explain. When I first knew William – or it might be more true to say when he first knew me – he had a cat, Tinkerbelle. She was a beautiful cat, a brindle tabby with an orange mark on her forehead. During most of the day, she would sleep, which was very comforting – see, there I go again – but then one day she killed a wren and brought it into the house. That was too much for William. Much as he was fond of Tinkerbelle, he loves the garden birds, and wrens are his favourites, by a long way his favourite. The killing of The Wren was more than he could bear and Tinkerbelle was banished, given away. Fortunately for her, she was given to a loving family with small children who apparently live in the middle of the countryside surrounded by open fields and woodland. William says she settled in within two weeks and is now as happy as can be. But I'm not. I miss her company, her just being there. Since she was sent away, William has more birds in the garden. That's true. Blue tits, great tits, coal tits and often a flock of long-tailed tits. They come to the bird feeders and they especially like the slabs of fat that he provides for them. There are a pair of robins, a pair of blackbirds and a pair of dunnocks. There is even a tree creeper with its creamy-white breast, and sometimes goldfinches. And then, just the other day, a new wren arrived and came to the threshold of the open door to let William know she was there. She will become The New Wren. Great delight!

Apart from all that, I live by myself, which is, of course, what we all do. Me and you. Even when we appear to be living with other people: husbands, wives, children, lovers, especially lovers, we live alone with them. Separate worlds sometimes touching each other. As you might suppose, being alone bothers William much more than me. I take the day as it comes. I have to, really. Like yesterday. We had breakfast, and I was just settled into the garden room with a book on snowdrops that I had picked up from the table by the sofa, when William walked in, evidently agitated.

"Abraham," he said, "you and I must have a talk."

I put the book down somewhat reluctantly as I had just begun to read about the many varieties of snowdrops and about a collection called 'Shakespeare's Ladies'. Fascinating. Did you know there are something like five thousand different varieties of snowdrop? And if you have a variety named after you – how nice would that be? – you are called 'an Immortal', and you get invited to lunch. Anyway, I put the book down so that we could talk.

"You see," said William, "although I have written you down, I'm not sure why I have created you."

I thought I might say that he hadn't created me, but had only summoned me up from a place deep within him and beyond him, but decided that would not be helpful. And so, I just looked surprised and asked him to say a bit more.

"Well, I don't know where you've come from. It's as if I arrived home one day and found you sitting here in the garden room looking out of the window, sitting here as if you had always been sitting here."

"Perhaps I have."

"And perhaps you haven't."

"Well, whichever it is," I said, hoping to move the conversation on, "perhaps we shouldn't worry too much about it. Perhaps, at least for now, we should just let it go, spend some time together and see where it goes."

William didn't reply, but just looked at me. He turned back towards his study, but before he left he said, "It's all very well for you to say that." Which is not entirely true, because when he makes me speak, I can only say what he already knows. And for the time being he knows less about me than you do.

William finds it difficult to let go. Once his mind is set on something – at the moment, what to do with me – he won't let it go. It will bother him. My mind is not like that at all. I flit from one thing to another, one moment this and then that. Flitting. Seems perfectly normal to me, but then I'm not trying to hold on to anything, especially happiness. I don't spend any time on that. William does, but I don't. For me, happiness is transient, unreliable and never quite enough, so I don't reach out for it. Instead, I try to find peace, to be *at peace*, to be at peace with myself and, most especially, to be at peace with the cosmos, which is, of course, a huge thing of which I am a tiny, very tiny, part. Where I come from, the world within and beyond, we know that this must be so. And, attached as I am to William, who is not at all peaceful, I find that trying to find peace takes up most of my time.

Now, there's another thing. Did you see that I said 'my time' as if there was a special bit of time that had been specifically given to me? I don't think that's very likely, do you? And anyway, I'm pretty sure that what we call 'time' is not really there. Isn't it true that most people believe that time is clockwork, tick, tick, tick, laid out in a straight line from a beginning to an end? And yet when I look around, at even small parts of the cosmos – I limit myself to the small parts – I notice something else, something more like a circle circling. Movement. Impermanence. That's the thing. Or rather, that's the no-thing. Don't you agree? But this is another part of being a fiction: although I can talk to you, I shall never know what you say in reply. I can imagine it, but I'll never know. All those conversations we could have about the patterns of the cosmos, and impermanence and whether William should have got rid of Tinkerbelle. I'll never hear them because we will never meet. I blame William for this.

Anyway, because William is caught in time, this time which doesn't really exist, he becomes fretful. He worries about becoming old, worries about becoming ill. He already has hearing aids and glasses and a rather persistent chesti-ness, which he treats by rubbing Vick onto his chest morning and night. And, shaping me in his own image, he wants to lay these things upon me too, including the Vick, which I'm not having. However much he might try, he cannot make it so. He may make me appear old, because that is what he has written, but, as you and I now know, this is just a theatrical show, a drama. Like actors being made to put on make-up and dress in pretend clothes for the parts that have been written for them. When the lights go up, what you see is a play and then, for a while, you are caught in it, believe in it. But it is just another fiction. Because, you see, I know something really important: (please note the colon, a pause) I have noticed that most people's lives are not dramatic. They are small and ordinary. They are made up of repeated tasks and events that take up most of their time – there we are with 'time' again. Ask any mother and she will tell you that, despite the women's revolution that is supposed to have set her free, she spends a great deal of her time simply making sure everything happens when it's meant to. A long list of seemingly endless chores which are very tiring and for which nobody says 'thank you'. And ask any man or woman at work. I'm pretty sure that you will find their days are not typically filled with momentous decisions and drama. Often they are tedious and unfulfilling.

Do you remember T S Eliot's *The Waste Land* and the crowd flowing over London Bridge? Well, it goes like this:

I had not thought death had undone so many.

and then,

And each man fixed his eyes before his feet.

Has much changed? I think not, although now each one of them would be holding a paper-fibre cup containing some kind of coffee from Starbucks, a caffè latte or perhaps a flat white or a caffè Americano. Whatever they are. The possibilities are almost endless, but please notice that every morning they will choose the same.

Sorry, got a bit carried away again. It's just that William is very fond of Eliot and so I often find books of his poetry lying around the house. And I've taken to reading them. *The Waste Land* and *Four Quartets*. They are wonderful, and I couldn't resist telling you about London Bridge.

So, here we are. And here I am. And you must see that even if he does not know it, in summoning up his dæmon, William has begun a quest, and the only way for him to proceed is to do just that. Proceed. I am here to help him, to go along with him. Be there, see where he takes us, and, without letting him know, help him to find the right pathway. You see – and I can only tell you this if you promise not to tell him – William's quest is not really about me. At the moment, that is what he thinks it is, but it is not. It is not about me. I am his companion, but that which he seeks is elsewhere. I cannot change his journey, I must follow him and play my part. He will shape the way, and I must follow and wear the clothes he gives me; sometimes I will guide him.

I'll tell you more about this, but let's talk later. It's been really nice meeting you.

CHAPTER TWO

G ood morning. Are you okay?
I meant to tell you that William is VERY worried about the weather. And I think you'd have to agree something is wrong. For example, out of nowhere, early this morning we had a torrential downpour of rain. Not just a heavy shower, but a torrent of wind and rain. It lasted half an hour and then stopped and went away. This seems to be happening more often. A week or two ago, the High Street in Aldeburgh experienced another downpour. Within an hour, shops and houses were flooded by the sheer volume of unmanageable water. And what about those hurricanes in America? The one that flooded Texas and the one that flooded Florida and then the other one. Climate change.

William takes these things seriously. He turns off lights that are left on needlessly, he composts and recycles, he refuses to buy vegetables in plastic wrapping and he has an electric car, a Renault Zoe that he calls 'Zoe'. Not original, but quite charming.

It is getting warmer isn't it? Everyone knows that, don't they? William says that as the ice melts it exposes the tundra (whatever that is) and this leads to a release of huge amounts of methane, which is not good. There is a vicious circle, he says. An initial warming leads to more emissions, which lead to more warming and more emissions. And…and apparently there may be a tipping point where a dreadful and self-reinforcing cycle takes over.

Ooops! I need to make some tea, although it is rather warm today.

CHAPTER THREE

I'm sitting in William's study. He's gone out. I think he has walked down to the Post Office. I've been left alone, so I've come in here to see what he's been working on. He's always working on something. As I have said before, William is not a very peaceful or calm person. Restless.

Anyway, here I am, and I'm just looking at a note that he has been writing. It's lying here on his worktop and it's all about, 'the essential nature of Modernity'. Wow! This is very William. Apparently, some people think that the modern world began about one or two hundred years ago with the wonders of the Industrial Revolution, the growth of science and the abandonment of God. But according to William's note, it all began a long time before that; it began not with scientists and industrialists but with theologians, mostly in Avignon. Yes, Avignon. It seems it was made worse by Martin Luther, who was evidently a very unhappy person. Anyway, all of these theologians and poor Martin Luther separated Divine Presence from Nature and made up a God who was unpredictable, unreliable and often rather cross. Well, that's what William has written down.

Men and women alike lost their place in the ordered cosmos and found themselves in chaos, desperately trying to become virtuous for their own salvation. But they were now on their own. God had left the Earth and taken up residence in the Sky...The dogma of Modernity was carried forward by Galileo, Bacon, Descartes and Hobbes, who raised Man (that means all of us) above what they now saw as a degraded Nature, which was to be bent to our will in order to serve God.

Thomas Hobbes, who was full of fear, was especially down in the dumps about it all. Poor Thomas.

I don't know why William worries himself about all of this. Perhaps he can't help it. Have *you* ever wondered how we've come to be where we are? You know, with bankers and footballers being paid so much you cannot imagine it, and with the Atlantic hurricanes growing in size and number. With the loss of curlews and the skylarks, and with global warming, and the people who say it can't be true. That's the kind of thing William worries about. He thinks we're headed towards 'a mighty catastrophe'.

Not being entirely of this world, I am rather less given to worrying. I'm more philosophical. I think that's what you would call it. More philosophical. Accepting things as they are, even if they're catastrophic, which I rather think they will be. When you dwell in the Cosmos as I do, you are inclined to see things in rather a different way. It's not that what happens close by is not important, on the contrary, it is: how we are with each other and how we care for each other and for the Earth is very important. It's just that much of what happens seems to be inevitable. Or to put it another way, when you dwell in the Cosmos it is easier to see that one thing must always lead to another. So, it's not much use complaining unless you tackle the underlying patterns of cause and effect. Change who you are. Become aligned to that which is good for all that is. The common good. The Cosmic good. Otherwise, catastrophe.

Anyway, where was I? Yes: how it is that we have come to be where we are, all that stuff about Modernity...That's the sort of thing William writes about. I'm not sure it's good for him.

CHAPTER FOUR

I have something I want to share with you. It's about knowing the sacred, or rather not being able to know it. The other day, I was sitting on a bench overlooking the sea, wrapped tightly in my long blue overcoat and a scarf, and wearing my woolly hat. It was a sunny day, though cold, and I had gone there to have my lunch. William was busy in his study. Not too far away. Anyway, while I was sitting on the bench a man came and sat beside me. I was surprised he could see me, but he could. William at work I suppose. Anyway, he smiled at me and said, "Good afternoon."

So, I said, "Good afternoon," and then I took from my bag a peanut butter and banana sandwich wrapped in greaseproof paper. Unwrapping the paper carefully, I took the sandwich and began to eat, slowly. Peanut butter and banana on sourdough bread. Excellent. But it has to be eaten slowly. By the way, I need to remind you that because I am a fiction, I can do anything I like – or at least anything William likes – even eat a peanut butter and banana sandwich slowly, which as you know, is delicious.

After a while, the man sitting beside me on the bench said, "Do you live here?" and I said I did and asked him if he was visiting. He said he was and that he was a Marketing Consultant, which sounded rather grand. Anyway, he said he had come to give advice to the local town council about 'putting Aldeburgh on the map'. I nodded.

I continued with my sandwich and then the Marketing Consultant turned to me and said, "It is rather wonderful isn't it?"

"It is," I said, unsure of whether the man was speaking of my sandwich or of the beach and the sea.

"It's part of the Aldeburgh 'brand'," he said. "It's what makes Aldeburgh 'it'."

"I imagine it must be," I said, realising that the man could not possibly be referring to my sandwich, which I had now finished, folding the greaseproof paper and putting it back in my coat pocket.

"Oh, yes," he said. "'It' is where it's all at."

"I suppose it must be," I said, now beginning to wish I was somewhere else. I looked out across the beach to the sea and the distant horizon, noting how sharp the edge was.

"Do you think I am right?" he asked.

"I suppose you must be," I said, not wanting to appear discourteous.

"So, what do *you* think?" he said abruptly.

"About what?" I replied, fearing that I must have upset him in some way. "What do I think about what?"

"About the beach and the sea," he said. "What do you think about the beach and the sea?"

"Oh," I said. Then I said nothing, until I said, "I think they are sacred."

"Sacred?" said the Marketing Consultant. "Sacred? What kind of word is that? Are you some kind of religious fanatic?"

I thought I might like to be some kind of a fanatic, but I knew that I was not, or at least that my days of being a fanatic must have long since passed. "No, I am not a fanatic," I said, somewhat reluctantly.

"Well, what do you mean then, when you say that the beach and the sea are sacred?"

"Well, I suppose what I mean is that they are part of something greater than you or me. I suppose that is what I must mean."

"Doesn't sound very likely to me," said the Marketing Consultant. "Doesn't sound very 'it'."

"No, I suppose not," I thought – but I decided not to say it out loud because it would have been wrong to do so. I did not want to upset the beach and the sea.

"I must be off now," I said, standing up and brushing the crumbs of the sandwich from my coat. "Goodbye." And I began to walk home.

As I left, I heard him say, "What an odd sort of a man. What a very odd sort of person indeed."

You see, he could not see the beach and the sea as sacred. He thought they were just what Aldeburgh had to offer. Part of its 'brand'. Something to be sold. And I guess that's how many other people would see it, too. But that's part of the problem isn't it? Don't you think so? It is why we cannot take care of each other and the sea. Why we find it difficult to love.

CHAPTER FIVE

I am really missing Tinkerbelle, but as I know William will not have her back, I am going to imagine a cat of my own. I can do that.

I have done so. Her name is Tabatha and she is a tabby. As soon as I imagine her, there she is, curled up asleep on a blanket on top of the blanket box in the living room, warmed by the morning sun. There she is. That feels better. All is well in the world.

CHAPTER SIX

Over the last few months, as winter has given way to spring, William and I have been getting to know each other. Or, I should say that he has been getting to know me, because I have always known him. It has been slow, and I think that at first, William was quite uncertain. But that has eased. It had to. Although I am part of who William is, he is not sure who I am, and he needs to know me better if we are to set off on an adventure. I know this is what he is thinking about because the other day when we were sitting in the garden room, drinking our tea, he told me he had been reading about the Grail Quest. You know, King Arthur and the Knights of the Round Table. He was telling me that each of the questing knights had to begin his journey in the darkest place of the forest. And William feels that this is where he is himself. In a dark place. *Courage, mon Brave!*

Anyway, today we are going to take a trip on the river in William's boat, *Springtide*. We started doing this as the weather began to warm and it has now become a regular thing for us. Part of the pattern of our life together. It is a sunny Sunday morning, but only one or two boats are out. The wind is quite strong and from the south, running upriver with the tide. The sky has two levels of cloud, an upper level of broken white clouds and a lower level of fast-moving grey clouds. There are patches of blue sky and I don't think it will rain. Because the wind is with the tide, there are no real waves, just a broken surface catching the sun's light.

As usual, the boatman from the Yacht Club has taken us out to *Springtide*, although he doesn't know that I'm here because, as usual, William has not introduced me and so I cannot be seen. *Springtide* is an old wooden workboat, larch on an oak frame with a wheel house made of iroko boards, and with windows around all sides to give a good view. You can open the ones to the front and the ones to the back. I think that's called the stern. I am becoming quite nautical!

Because the wind is from the south with a touch of east and we want to sail southwards down river, William will keep the front window and the door on the windward side, the left hand side, the port side, closed. Snug. I'm getting used to this boat.

Soon we have hoisted the burgee on the aft mast, turned on the engine and let go of the mooring. We drop back until we can see the mooring in front of us and then we steer away around it and move forward, slowly at first. As the engine warms, William opens the throttle until, against the tide, we are making a good four knots. We are clear of the moored boats and William lets me take over. I open up the throttle some more, five knots. The tide is low but rising. On either side, there are mud banks that will soon be covered by the river. There are a few waders, picking their way through the mud, and I keep to the side, pushing into the tide where it is less strong, watching the depth on the depth sounder.

There is something special about letting go of the mooring. Letting go and feeling the flow of the tide; feeling the direction of the wind, which today is strong, but not cold. It's mesmerising. I enter another world, and I think William does, too. An ancient sense of adventure and possibility mixed with fearfulness. We take *Springtide* downriver towards Orford. We go as far as the old communications buildings set amidst tall radio masts on the seaward shore. Then we turn. And now, running with the tide and with the wind behind us, I cut back the throttle and let the river carry us, opening the front window, now sheltered from the wind.

We are only out for an hour and a half, but in that time we are transformed by the river. We have felt the taste of freedom. As we come back to the Yacht Club, there are two small sailing dinghies in difficulty. One has a broken mast and the other is floating upside down in the river, the rescue boat holding on whilst the crew climb aboard. We watch as they try to bring the boat upright, which eventually they do.

We take *Springtide* beyond her mooring and then turn her into the tide, edging forwards to pick up the loop of the mooring rope that floats on the surface of the water. Because I have done this before, I know what has to be done. William takes the wheel and I pick up the mooring rope with the mooring pole, placing the loop of the rope over the post in the foredeck. The tide and the wind are pushing us back and I feel the weight of *Springtide* straining against the post. We have already left another rope around the post and now I slip its end through the loop of the mooring rope, and make it fast. I then release it so that it is slack, easing the loop and the mooring rope away. Pushing the throttle slightly forward, William lets *Springtide* once more edge towards the buoy. He slips the throttle into neutral and I move forward and position the slack rope through the jaws on the prow. Then I pull the mooring rope back up through the jaws and once more slip the loop onto the post, unfolding the other rope and setting it aside on the foredeck, for the next time. We are done. William cuts the engine and all is quiet.

Now there are ropes to be tidied, the battery to be turned off, the burgee to be taken down. Windows to be closed and the doors of the wheelhouse to be locked. We wait for the boatman to come and take us ashore, although, again, he only sees William. As I said before, William has never introduced me to the boatman. Just hasn't bothered. He's like that. I think, at the moment, he fears that if he does not hold me close, he might lose me. You see, he cannot reconcile the Abraham he has created in his imagination, the 'me' who enables him to express those things that he struggles with, and the 'me' who holds the mooring rope. I know, it is a bit tricky isn't it? But there it is. We are all multiple manifestations of ourselves.

Anyway, none of this matters today. Today, I, Abraham Soar, am at peace.

CHAPTER SEVEN

Yesterday evening I was sitting in the garden room with Tabatha when William came in with a tray of tea. William, who by the way cannot see Tabatha, gave me my cup, sat down and began talking about 'being peaceful'. Apparently, that morning he'd had a Skype call with some people who are writing a book about it. Imagine that, writing a book about being peaceful. As if we can't be peaceful without reading a book about it! Anyway, this discussion was on William's mind and I could feel that he wanted to tell someone about it, and I was to be his audience. So, having trapped me in the garden room with a cup of tea, he began to speak about the nature of peacefulness.

"You know, Abraham," he said, in a voice that meant I was to listen, "finding that 'peace' within us is really important."

This is the sort of thing that William *says*. He says he loves peace and stillness and silence, but most of the time he isn't peaceful at all. Most of the time he is on the phone or travelling up to London, or checking his emails. He writes about it. Writes about it all the time, but he doesn't *do* it. Not at all. There is a break, a gap, between what he says and what he does. And I think that this is partly why I'm here. Why he has summoned me. Somehow, although I doubt he can express it – not for the moment – somehow, he knows that if he is to find peace he has to have me beside him. He suspects that Abraham Soar, this part of him he hardly knows, can show him the way.

Anyway, he starts talking about his book, and he says that he thinks people are no longer attracted to stillness and silence. Perhaps he is right. Perhaps most people aren't. But I am. And so is Tabatha. Sometimes, when I'm on my own in the house, when only Tabatha and I are here, I feel the stillness around me as if it were a cloak, and I hear the silence as if it were the breath of eternity. And when this happens I am not sure where the border is between myself and the Cosmos. I slip between the two. Sometimes in the silence I feel that my body is not mine at all. I look at my bare feet as if they belong to someone else. And then I 'slip' and am taken up in the air, the wind, the sunshine and the rain. It's an odd feeling, but there it is. When this happens, nothing seems to matter – especially matter!

Is this what William wants to find? I wonder.

CHAPTER EIGHT

William has been away in London and I am waiting for him to get back. There is something I want to ask him. As usual, while he was away I didn't have much to do, so I went into his study to see what he'd been up to. His desk was covered with books and papers, and lying beside the keyboard to his iMac, was a scrap of paper on which he had written two words, 'Love' and 'Fear'. He's like that. Words, words, words and more words. His head is full of them and I think they matter more to him than I do. Although, of course, without words, he couldn't bring me to life.

Anyway, there was this scrap of paper with the words 'Love' and 'Fear' written on it. I had been thinking about taking a nap, but once I had read these words I couldn't stop thinking. Just by leaving that piece of paper there for me to find, William had made me think about what he had written, and then I couldn't get the words out of my head. Thank you William. Just as I was about to put my feet up and close my eyes, you filled my head with your words. 'Love' and 'Fear'.

And then, of course, I started to look at the other books and papers on the desk, and I found a book called *The Myth of the Goddess*. It was open at a page which described the Greek goddess Aphrodite. Apparently, as the symbol of Beauty and Renewal she was born out of the foam of Love and gave birth to three children, Harmonia, Deimos and Phobos – Harmony, Terror and Fear. So, perhaps that's what he was going to write about, something about the kinship of Love and Fearfulness. When he comes back, I'm going to ask him. I want to know what's troubling him. I think I know, but I need to hear it from him. You see, for the time being I can only know what he tells me. I can only be what he writes down. This will change. But that's not where we are. Not yet.

William arrived home about a quarter of an hour ago and I made him some tea and toast. We are sitting at the table in the living room, and he has been telling me about how the train to Ipswich ran late and how he nearly missed the connection to Saxmundham. He is pleased to be home.

"While you were in London," I say, "I was looking at the papers on your desk. I hope you don't mind."

"No, I don't," says William. "And anyway, I assume that's what you do."

"Well, we are trying to get to know one another aren't we?"

"That's true."

"So," I say, "I was reading what you have been writing about Love and Fear."

"And?"

"And I have been wondering where this Fear comes from?"

William finishes his toast and picking up his cup goes to sit in one of the armchairs. I stand up and follow him, taking the other armchair, so that we are now facing each other across the room. He looks at me and takes a gulp of his tea. I have a feeling he is going to talk *at* me. He often does this. I think the distance between our two armchairs helps him.

"Do you remember," he says, "what it was like before you were born? You know, what it was like in your mother's belly, floating in the warmth and security of her womb. Connected. And can you remember the shock of birth? Being pushed out into a world. Suddenly becoming separate."

I'm rather cross about this because, as William must know, I have no memory at all of such things. And even if he doesn't know where I have come from, he must know that he has not given me a past. I suppose he's just forgotten, or rather I think he is now making a speech and so it doesn't matter. His audience is elsewhere.

"No wonder we start life frightened," he says. "And as we do, it's no wonder we need as much love and comfort as we can get. We want to be loved, want to be made whole again."

What he has just said is very important, because when he says '*we* want to be loved', I very much suspect he means, '*I* want to be loved'. Hold onto that. Remember it: he thinks we need, or he needs, as much love and comforting as we can get.

Anyway, he is now in full flight.

"With a bit of luck, when we are born, we will be gathered up and held to our mother's breast. But not all of us. Some of us *are* loved well and when this happens we learn to cope with being apart, being on our own. But for a lot of us, that separation, that fearfulness, is where it all starts going wrong."

He stops for a moment as if he has just thought of something. Then he continues. I'm just listening. Nothing else is required of me. Or Tabatha, who is asleep.

"I once knew someone who suffered this terribly. When she was born, she was left to lie there beside her mother until the midwife came. Perhaps it was not long, but she told me that it felt like forever. And she never quite recovered. Never felt comforted. It was too late – the damage had been done. The hurt was never mended and she never forgave her mother. And I think her mother never forgave her, either. I suppose they were both frightened."

Again he pauses.

"The irony was that she died before her mother, and even in her death, her mother was not with her."

He stops talking and looks out of the window into the garden as if he is remembering something. There is something here that he cannot quite catch. Then he continues, once more talking to himself rather than to me, turning over in his mind what he is saying so that, later, no doubt, he can write it down.

"I have often wondered why it is we remain fearful. And perhaps this is it: when we are born, we have to separate to become fully alive, but then we spend the rest of our lives yearning to become one again. And so, we begin a lifelong search. We look for it in romantic love, and we look for it in good companionship. But some of us never find the love and never lose the fear, and so it catches us out at three o'clock on a summer's afternoon when someone who we hope loves us fleetingly turns their back, pulls away, just because they're tired. It catches us out, and before we can help it we are frightened and strike out with a remark, with a gesture, with a look, with that tone in our voice. We don't mean to, but we do. And then it's too late. The damage has been done, at least for a while. It might be just that day or it might be for several days. Horrid. Full of hurtfulness and sadness and regret."

Again he stops and I wonder what all of this has been about. I know that however many words he uses, he is talking of himself, and that this explains why he never lets anyone come too close. In case they turn their back and walk away.

I stroke Tabatha's head and she begins to purr. There is one more thing he wants to tell me, or tell himself; make a note of it for himself.

"You know, I was once told by someone called Four Arrows, that the indigenous people of North America, the First Nations people, regard fear as a *necessary* quality, because it enables us to recognise danger and then to summon the courage to face up to it and take whatever action is needed to deal with it. Without fear, they say, we cannot see the threat for what it is. What it truly is. And, he said that our problem now is that because we no longer understand the purpose of fear, we fail to see the very thing that really threatens us: a harmful form of economy that wants us always to be consuming more. It should be as frightening as a very large grizzly bear, but we don't see it, cannot see it. And so, we don't summon up the courage to face up to it. The consequence is all about us – and not feeling the fear as a warning, not seeing the threat, and not summoning the courage, is dangerous. It may be our undoing."

He lets out a deep sigh, stands up and walks into his study, closing his door behind him. I know that he is often frightened.

CHAPTER NINE

You know when you wake up in the morning and the house is quiet and still? You pull back the curtains and stand by the window, looking out at the beginning of the day. In this early daytime, the garden is also quiet and still. It's spring, and nothing seems to be moving. It's as if the whole of Being is waiting. Waiting to come alive. Of course, elsewhere, in other places, people are up and about, cars and lorries are at work, there is noise and action. But here, in this particular moment, in this place, in this very particular part of the Cosmos, it is still. There is no time, no age, only stillness. And you cannot speak. Your voice will not come. Quite alone.

It was just like that this morning. I was in my dressing gown, the warm one, dark blue. As the day was waiting to begin, I waited, too. I walked through to the kitchen and made a pot of tea. Just a small pot, with my cup. Of all of William's cups, this is my favourite. It is white and squat, and according to William it's called 'a morning cup' and was made by a wonderful artist, Karen Downing. Apparently, she used to live nearby, but now lives in the Brecklands of west Norfolk. All her work is white. Bowls, cups and plates, tableware. Hand thrown porcelain. All white. William has quite a lot of her work, but the morning cup is my favourite. It has straight sides and a flat bottom, on which there is a swirl. The cup is not quite round. Each of her cups is, in its own particular way, not quite round. Perfect. I don't think this one would like to be anywhere else but here in this morning, in this quietness.

CHAPTER TEN

Dear reader, I have made a decision. I must talk to William. I need to talk to him about what we might expect from each other. I may exist because of him, but in spirit I am utterly free. And although he needs me as much as I need him, sometimes I long for places he cannot imagine.

And here is something. Because I live in William's imagination, deep within, I know him quite well, and I have noticed from what he has told me and from what I have seen that he doesn't have many deep friendships with men in his life. Less than a handful. Maybe only one or two. He prefers the company of women. But here's the paradox: he likes their company, but only so far. A week or so ago, quite unexpectedly, he asked a woman he had only recently met if she would like to go on holiday with him. Her name is Marianne. She said 'yes,' and a week later they flew to Portugal and stayed in a hotel north of Oporto. Separate rooms. Apparently, it was a rather lovely hotel with well-kept grounds and a couple of swimming pools. Very quiet, with walks along the coast and suppers in a local restaurant that, apart from local dishes, had a good vegetarian menu. They talked a lot about their lives. She is a painter and took her sketchbook, sitting on the beach or in the gardens, drawing, and he took his journal with him, each day trying to write down exactly what was in front of him. One morning he thought he saw me sitting at a nearby table at the restaurant under an umbrella, with a plate of cheese and olives, drinking the local wine and just looking around. I seemed very content. But once he put away his journal and looked again, I had gone. And then Marianne came back from the beach and showed him her sketches. They stayed for three days and then flew back to Stansted. They drove back to Aldeburgh and he dropped Marianne off at her house before coming home.

I was waiting for him. Sitting on a chair in the garden, my eyes closed under my wide-brimmed Panama hat, my hands resting on my belly. I was asleep, but as William walked up the path, I woke and smiled at him. I think he was pleased to be back.

"How did you get on?" I said.

"It was fine," he said.

"Is this the beginning of a great romance?"

"No, I don't think so."

"Oh!"

We both laughed.

"We could have some supper," he said.

"That would be nice," I said. "I was wondering whether I would get to eat today."

And so we sat and had supper together. Just cheese on toast.

"How was Portugal, then? Sunny?"

"Yes, sunny and warm. Every day, sunny and warm, but with a breeze off the sea."

"Which was good?"

"Yes, which was good."

We sat in silence for a while. Then he said, "You know Abraham, I'm not sure I'm very competent in my relationships with women."

Competent, that was an odd word.

"Well," I said, "I've decided to have no gender."

"What on earth do you mean?"

"While you were away, I looked up some websites on your computer. Apparently, it is becoming common amongst young people not to refer to their gender. In order finally to break away from the old prejudices about men and women, they claim no gender at all. It's as if a future with less separation between men and women is calling them. So, I have decided to do the same. It makes me very 'of the moment'. I now regard myself as being pan-gender. I am both man and woman. Or neither."

"That is going to make it very difficult for me, isn't it? How shall I refer to you?"

"Just as Abraham," I said.

"Well, we will have to see," he said. "I am not at all sure I want this. Let's talk about it later."

So, here we are. It's four o'clock and William and I are sitting together having tea in the garden room.

"Abraham," he says, "I want to talk to you about this matter of gender. You know, you deciding to be pan-gender, or whatever you call it."

"Well, it's your fault. You made me do it."

"Did I?"

"Yes, of course you did. How else could I have thought about it? It is probably something you are wondering about, but making me say."

"Well, I am not sure I can go along with it. I enjoy the 'differences'. I like women. Generally, I like them more than men. And, I'm having some difficulty in seeing everyone as being the same."

"Well, you got me thinking about it."

"Well, maybe. And I can see what young people are saying; that if we are to rebalance our world, nurture it, we have to give expression to qualities which are different from those that arise in cultures dominated by men."

He was off. Thinking.

"So, what are you going to do about it?" I say.

"I have no idea, but you have made me think, and so earlier this afternoon when I was filling in an online form for a new electricity account I selected 'prefer not to say' when I was asked my gender. That's a start."

"Well done, William. But you could have written, 'Why are you asking me this?'"

"I suppose so."

For a while neither of us speaks.

"Well, I'm finding this rather tiring," I say. "Perhaps, at my age, I should let others decide; just keep out of their way. Yes, I'll just keep out of their way. 'Their' is alright isn't it? Gender free? Anyway, my world is yours to command."

"It doesn't always seem to work like that."

"No, not always. What do you think about wearing lipstick? Bright red?"

"Oh, for heaven's sake Abraham! I don't think about such things at all."

And he stands up and is about to walk out of the room when I say, "William, don't go. I have something I want to talk about."

He turns, and for a moment looks at me as if he is not sure whether or not to stay.

"Just sit with me for a while."

He looks at me again and then returns to the sofa.

"Well, what is it?" he says.

"It's about you and me, and where I have come from."

"Go on."

"You probably think I am nothing more than someone you have made up, someone you have created by writing me down."

"Well, that's true isn't it? I don't remember you being here before." He looks uneasy.

"But I was always here, William. It's just that you couldn't see me. Not until you placed me on the page."

This is getting difficult for him. He sits forward and places the palms of his hands on his knees.

"Look," he says, "I am pretty sure that until I wrote your name on the first page, you were not there."

"But I was. I have always been here, William. Within you and beyond you."

William stands up and walks to the window, looking out towards the garden, his back to me.

"You see, William, I come from another place." He turns, his arms folded across his chest in self-defence. "I am your spirit: everything you are, have been and could be. Ageless, timeless. You just called me forth. In placing me here in this place, in these clothes, you have brought me into a kind of being. One which you recognise. But I've always been here."

"So, let me get this straight," he says. "You have always been part of me and I just called you forth? But why?"

"Well, that, my dear William, is what we have to discover. But if I were a gambling man – which actually, I am – I would put money on Love."

"Love? What do you mean?"

"It's the thing that limits you, William. Not knowing how to love and be loved. And I'm pretty sure you brought me here to find your way towards it."

William looks away from me and towards the garden, where a small flock of long-tailed tits are clustered around the feeder. I had hit the spot, but he could not admit it. He wanted to, but he couldn't. But I think that although he couldn't say it, he knew he had called me forth. He knew he had brought me into being to help him find love. He was writing me, because he needed me to show him the way. And now he was ready to take the first step.

PART TWO

BRYONY

CHAPTER ELEVEN

Sometimes the task of being who William wishes me to be is claustrophobic. In order to breathe, I have to unbutton my collar. Take off my socks. Loosen. Loosen. That feels better.

CHAPTER TWELVE

If I am to help William in his quest for Love, he needs to find someone for me to love. Since William brought me to the pages of this book, I have had no relationships at all. That must change. I need to love and be loved.

No sooner has this thought come into my head than, of course, William has the same thought. Or was it the other way round? I am in the kitchen with the fridge door open looking for something to eat when he walks in.

"I am wondering, Abraham," he says, "whether you might like a friend? Living alone with me must be a bit dull. What do you think?"

"As you already know," I say, "I would like that."

"Well, I have someone I would like to introduce you to. Her name is Bryony Sanders. She is just the sort of woman you would like."

Or he would like. And I am wondering what sort of woman that would be.

It's only a day or two later and William is taking me to meet Bryony. She lives just along the road in Thorpeness. Apparently, she was a dancer, but now she has retired and has come to live by the sea. William says that she is looking forward to meeting me. He would say that, wouldn't he?

We arrive at Bryony's house just before eleven o'clock in the morning. It is one of a row of holiday houses built on what is called Sandy Bar, the Thorpeness dune overlooking the North Sea, facing east toward the open sea, a long shingle beach running north-south. The house is long and low, weatherboarded and painted off-white, with a veranda at the front, the roof is pan-tiled. It backs onto a sandy dirt road. To the side is a separate building that was once a garage. It looks as if it has been converted to provide accommodation for guests. We park behind the house and walk round to the front. William knocks on the door and Bryony opens it, welcoming us and inviting us in.

We walk into a large living room, the ceiling following the line of the sloping roof up into the rafters. It has windows overlooking the sea, and they look as if they might fold back on a warm day so that the room and the veranda become one space. Wonderful. Two armchairs and a sofa with a low table between them made of driftwood. On the table is a bowl of oranges. No curtains at the windows, just simple plain white linen roller blinds. And on the wooden floor a large and ancient rug frayed at the edges, probably from a holiday in Turkey. A chest of drawers with a mirror and photos on it, family photos. The kitchen is at the back of the house, but opens directly into the living room, and then there are two doors to what I assume must be Bryony's bedroom and bathroom, both of which appear to run along the southern side of the house. There is a staircase which, as I discover later, leads up to an attic bedroom and bathroom with a round window overlooking the sea.

"Bryony, this is Abraham." says William. "Abraham, this is Bryony."

We smile at each other.

"I am going to leave you two together while I go to Waitrose. I'll call back later."

"Okay," says Bryony.

As soon as Bryony opened the door to her house and invited us in, I knew I would like her. She has that elegant way of standing that dancers have; balanced, upright, as if they might at any moment spin round on one toe. She is dressed in light blue overalls over a flowery blouse, no shoes. I like no shoes. Her hair is wild, blonde and curly, and it is decorated with a hair slide of golden yellow. She smells of the sea and of cloves. Very slightly of cloves. Very attractive.

"Take a seat," she says. "Would you like some tea?"

"Yes please."

"Sit here."

And so, I sit down in an armchair while Bryony goes into her kitchen, returning with a tray set with colourful cups and saucers, a large brown tea pot and a blue jug of milk. Sky blue. She pushes the bowl of oranges to one side and puts the tray on the table between us. Then walking back into her kitchen she come backs with a plate of chocolate digestive biscuits.

"So, here we are," says Bryony. "And in a way we are kin."

"What do you mean?"

"Well, neither of us would be here if it was not for William, would we?"

"I suppose not, although it doesn't always feel like that."

"What do you mean?"

I wonder how much I can tell her. I choose caution. "Well, of course, as I am sure you must know, we are only here because of William, his writing. But there are moments when I do not feel that he is writing me at all. I feel as if I dwell somewhere else and am just giving him some of my time. But then it fades."

"I don't think I have ever thought of that, Abraham. But now I will keep an eye open for it. Even you talking about it feels rather exciting!"

She pours tea with what I feel must be the elegance of a dancer. And as she does so, I feel certain that we shall come to know each other well.

"Do you live by yourself, Abraham?" she says.

"No, not really. I live with William, and I have an imaginary cat called Tabatha."

"An imaginary cat?"

"Yes. William had a cat, Tinkerbelle, but he got rid of her and so I had to imagine another one."

"That's very odd."

We laugh.

"I suppose it is. And you, Bryony, do you live by yourself?"

"Yes I do. Well, I do now." She pauses. "For some reason, I seem to have become very comfortable in my own company."

"I can imagine that," I say, "if you don't mind me saying so."

Again, we laugh. How strange it is. We have not met before, but already we seem to be at ease. There is something almost serene about her. She has presence, as if she holds the space between us. I suppose a dancer would do that, wouldn't she?

We sit and have our tea. I am looking at the sea, which today is calm, and Bryony opens the front door and suggests we sit on the veranda, which we do. I like verandas and this one is lovely; two rattan armchairs with blue and cream striped cushions. Bryony tells me about Thorpeness and the people who live there. Lots of them are holiday makers, but there is a small community of people who live there all the time, and now she is one of them. She tells me about being a dancer, how much she loved it. She trained at the Royal School of Ballet and danced at Covent Garden.

"And then, because I was young and wanted to be 'free' – whatever that is – I accepted an invitation, and then one invitation after another, to dance in musicals in America and London. I loved it! I danced for over fifteen years."

"And then?"

"And then I was too old. Dancing is very demanding, physically. Not many dancers in the theatre do so for much more than fifteen years. I danced until I was nearly thirty-five. Not bad really."

We drink our tea and I look at her, beautiful as she is, and I imagine her aged twenty-two.

"Did you stay in the theatre?"

"For a while. It's a difficult place to leave, and because I was known both in London and New York I was offered work helping with choreography and managing the young dancers, taking care of them I suppose. But of course, it's not the same. When you stop dancing, you die a little."

She looks away from me.

"And then I met Jonathan, married him and had two children all within five years. That answered the question of what I should do!"

We laugh, and Bryony collects our cups and takes them into the kitchen. I like her laughter. She comes back.

"But I was lucky," she says. "Again, because I knew people, I was asked by an American magazine, *Stage and Dance*, if I would review London shows. It was great. About twice a month, I would go to a new musical or a new show and then write a review. I was able to interview dancers, directors and theatre people. I loved it. Until it ended."

"Until it ended?"

She looks at her hands, splaying out her fingers as if she is examining her nails. She wears a thin gold wedding band on the ring finger of her left hand.

"Would you like to walk?" she says.

"Yes, let's walk."

The tide is out and we walk along the hard sand at the water's edge. At one point, Bryony takes my arm. Just for a moment or two. And then she lets it go and we turn and walk back. Just before we reach the house Bryony stops and looks out across the sea towards the horizon, as if she is gazing at something now in the distance.

"Jonathan died a couple of years ago, just after we had bought this house. We had planned to use it for holidays. He was retiring and I had agreed to retire as well, or at least to ease up. But that was not to be, and when Jonathan died I came here to recover. All our plans for being together had been broken."

She pauses.

"And now I couldn't go back to London. I just couldn't. I think I never will. I am managing, just about, but sometimes the hurt is raw. And I miss the small things. The just being together. God, I miss that."

"I'm sorry," I say.

"Me too," she says.

We walk up to the house and I notice that what was the garage has the words 'Guest House' carved on a wooden panel and painted blue above the front door. As we step up onto the veranda, William returns.

We say our goodbyes, hoping we will see each other again.

Although I am only a fiction, I know what love is. Gender or no gender, that is not what matters. And, of course, as I have told you, that is why I am here. William has such difficulty with love, or more precisely, with being loved, by accepting that he is loved, feeling loved. I know that nothing to do with love is ever straightforward, but as far as I can tell, William is quite a long way from understanding it at all. You see, he always keeps a distance, a step or two back, and I have wondered whether this is because he doesn't actually know how to be loved. He recently met someone he really liked. Do you remember, they went to Portugal together? If he had made a list – and he likes lists – if he had made a list of all the things he liked in a woman, she would have matched up very well. But he didn't, and so they didn't. Somehow, he couldn't see that she was loving him. It was as if no matter how much she loved him, it was never enough for him to feel it.

Anyway, as a being of spirit I like to love and be loved, and I can easily imagine it with Bryony. Suppose I got to know her, really know her. I can imagine us spending time together, going for walks along the beach, perhaps having tea in the tea-shop in Thorpeness or here in William's house. She could come here and we could walk across the marshes and along the river wall...

Imagine this: Bryony has driven over from Thorpeness to see me and we are having lunch together at the Brudenell Hotel on Crag Path, overlooking the shingle beach and the sea. Yes, this is just right. The sea is rough, large waves crashing down onto the shingle, drawing back and crashing again. The wind, blowing from the south, is skimming the spray from the top of the waves, spindrift. Bryony has ordered the fish of the day, hake, and I have ordered a vegetarian lasagne. Two glasses of wine, white for Bryony and red for me. Large glasses, I think. We are sitting by the dining room window and so have a good view of the sea, Bryony looking north and me south. I like this. When we have had our lunch, we decide to walk along the coastal Crag Path, northwards past the fishermen's shacks selling fish, some of which will have been caught that day by the boats that are launched from the beach, and then on towards the northern end of the town, to where there is an open water meadow and marshes, North Warren, with pools of standing water, cattle grazing. The wind has been behind us, but now as we turn to walk back it is in our faces. Strong. And we laugh and bend into it until, at last, our eyes watering, we come to the cinema and then the town steps and make our way up from the High Street and back to William's house, my house. We have found it easy to talk. Not about anything really special, but about living by the sea and Bryony's life as a dancer. We have agreed that we will meet again.

Suppose all that had happened.

CHAPTER THIRTEEN

Now William is cross with me.

"I wish you wouldn't do that," he says, "taking your life into your own hands and imagining things that I'm not ready for."

"I'm sorry," I say. Of course, I'm not really sorry. He must know that.

He shakes his head.

"Well, I suppose it's my fault. I introduced you to Bryony. But I wasn't ready for you to take her out to lunch. I'm not sure what it was that I was supposing, but not that. Now what do I do?"

"The lunch was just a fantasy," I say. "It didn't really happen. Although I should have liked it if it had."

"Well, you have clearly begun to get to know each other, be with each other. And now you've agreed to meet each other again. How can I change that? Of course, I *can*. But then, of course, I *cannot*. I think I'm stuck with it."

"I suppose so," I say.

William looks at me.

"I'm fond of you, Abraham. I like your company. I even like you living with me. But when you do something I hadn't expected, I don't know whether to be upset or relieved. Angry or fascinated."

I say nothing.

"Well, I didn't really invent you did I?" he says. "You just came to me, pretty much fully formed. As if you had always been there. Which you hadn't, although you say you had. Anyway, today I have things to do that do not concern you at all."

He stands up and walks into his study.

CHAPTER FOURTEEN

This morning, I received a card in the post. It was lying on the mat in the hall when I came through for breakfast. It is a picture of the reed beds at the bird sanctuary at Minsmere, just up the coast, and it shows a curlew flying low over the reeds. It is from Bryony. She has invited me to go for a walk and has said she can come and pick me up in her car. She has written her phone number on the card.

I don't get many invitations. Actually, I don't get any. So, this is very special, and as I read it, I straighten my hair and check that my fly is not open, as if she was walking up the path towards me. I'll ring her on the phone in the hall.

"Hello Bryony it's me."

"Me?"

"Me, Abraham."

"Oh, hello Abraham. Did you get my card?"

"Yes, that's why I'm calling you. I would love to go for a walk with you."

"Good. What day would suit you? I was thinking of picking you up at about ten-thirty."

"Sounds good. How about tomorrow?"

"Works for me."

"Okay, I'll be ready tomorrow at ten-thirty."

"See you then."

Do you see what happens, William, when you open yourself to love? Or at least friendship, which is a kind of love.

I think I might have to talk to Tabatha about this. Where is she? Oh, there she is, lying on a blanket on one of the armchairs in the garden room. As I walk in she remains asleep, but one ear twitches as if she has heard something – me. I stroke her head gently and as I do so, she opens her eyes, lifts one paw and uncurls herself revealing her soft cream underbelly.

"The thing is, Tabatha," I say, "I don't quite know how this thing with Bryony will go."

Tabatha yawns.

"I think I'm nervous about it, but I'm not quite sure why."

I don't know what I am expecting from an imaginary cat, but Tabatha turns back on to her stomach and tucks her front paws under her cream throat and chest. She looks at me, and then, to my surprise, for she has never spoken before, she says,

"It is well known that cats are rather particular about relationships. As I am with you."

I am about to speak, but she continues.

"Just listen. The first aspect of a good relationship is functional. Cats like people who feed them and give them shelter, although this is somewhat problematic in our case since, as I am no more than a part of your imagination, being fed is notable by its absence. This aspect may not be a significant part of your relationship with Bryony, although she has already provided you with tea. The second aspect of a good relationship for a cat is companionship. In a way, we are companions, and you are for the most part an agreeable person to be with – as far as people go. This matter of companionship may be very important in your relationship with Bryony. Inhabiting as I do the rich domains of your imagination, I would say that some of your fantasies about her might be far-fetched – you know, her elegance, the smell of cloves. I think I know where that is going. But if you can behave properly, you and she could become good companions. And since you have met and she is now inviting you to meet her again, we can assume that you have a chance."

Tabatha stands up and stretches, raising her rear haunches and stretching out her front legs. Then she sits up and looks away from me towards the window. She has clearly tired of our conversation.

"I suppose we could go for a walk," I say. "I shall keep my fantasies in check, but it is true, I do find Bryony physically attractive. Very much so."

At this, Tabatha walks out of the room, her tail held high. She has had enough.

The following day at just after ten-thirty, Bryony arrives at William's house. William has gone to London for the day. I had not said anything to him about this visit and I was therefore not certain that it would happen. Unless, of course, he already knew about it and was writing it down.

Bryony comes up the garden path. She walks so gracefully I am taken aback. Then I remember what Tabatha said. Behave yourself, Abraham. Bryony is wearing a dress patterned with blossoms, reds and blues on a cream background, a lavender coloured cardigan over her shoulders and a pair of yellow high-heeled shoes. She looks lovely, her curly hair catching the sunlight. We greet each other with a kiss on both cheeks.

"I hope you don't mind," she says, "but I've changed our plans. As I was having breakfast this morning, I thought that instead of just going for walk we could drive to Orford and have a hot chocolate at the Pump Street Bakery. I've only been once before, but their hot chocolate is especially chocolatey. And they make wonderful croissants."

"I am in your hands," I say.

Had William really supposed that such a thing was possible? Hot chocolate and croissants? Apparently, he had.

We drive to Orford, crossing the river at Snape, through the Tunstall forest and open fields, some of which are growing nothing more than turf, just a carpet of short grass. A huge lawn ready to be cut, rolled up and taken away. Through Sudbourne, with its village hall and Post Office, we arrive at Orford and park in the town square – well, it's not really a square, more like an open space for cars. There is the Pump Street Bakery and inside the soft smell of warm bread. We order two of their especially intense chocolate drinks – chocolate beans from Ecuador – and two croissants, finding a place to sit on a long table in the room next to the shop.

During the drive we caught up with what was happening in our lives – not much – and talked about the countryside through which we were passing. Just pleasant chatting, Bryony sitting somewhat upright at the steering wheel and me almost horizontal. For some reason, the passenger seat had been reclined, my head being only just above the dashboard. I had put on my straw Panama and was wearing sunglasses. Now, sitting at the table, I ask Bryony why she had chosen to come to Orford.

"It was just a spur of the moment thing," she says. "I like the drive through the Tunstall forest, and I am very fond, more than fond, of this chocolate drink."

The chocolate is exceptionally good. It tastes dark, bitter and strong. I break off one end of my croissant and bite into the fluffy pastry. Excellent. Bryony has done the same and now we smile at each other, our mouths full of deliciousness.

"I was talking about you yesterday," I say.

"Really? Who were you talking to?"

"I was talking to Tabatha."

"Tabatha? Your imaginary cat?"

"Yes."

"What on earth were you talking about?"

"I was asking her about relationships."

"Is that something cats know about?"

I don't think she really thought I had been talking to Tabatha.

"Oh, yes. According to Tabatha, cats have a very particular sense of relationship. And she explained to me that for a cat, companionship is the most important aspect of being in a relationship. They place it above affection, although of course companionship is a form of affection, don't you think?"

"Yes I do. I've had quite a lot of 'relationships' as you're calling them, but those that have worked best for me have always been ones in which I felt I was with a companion, someone who liked us being together. My late husband Jonathan, for example. Especially him. But then we were lovers as well as companions. There was no boundary between us – well, only sometimes. We moved easily between the different dimensions of our intimacy, from one world to another. Some parts were very private and small and others were vast and open. Sometimes we wanted to be 'out there' with friends and family, and sometimes it was as if we'd lost touch with everything but ourselves. Let slip. Have you ever done that?"

I don't reply, but she looks at me as if she hopes that I know what she is talking about.

"Bryony," I say, "do you mind if I ask you how old you are?"

"Not at all. I'm sixty something. Early sixties. And you?"

"I have no age."

"No age?"

"Not really. I think William wants me to be seventy something. But I'd settle for sixty-five. For today, anyway."

I drink the last mouthful of my chocolate and spoon out the dregs from the bottom of the cup. Very satisfying.

"What do you think William wants of us?" she asks.

I pretend that I don't know. "I'm not sure, and I don't think he is either. But I think he has brought us into his life to help him in some way, and now he wonders what will happen."

"So, this morning… is this William or us?"

"Either and both."

We finish our croissants and then I realise I have no money. Fortunately Bryony has.

"Let's leave the car here and walk down to the Quay," she says.

So we do, and Bryony takes my arm, which I like. Her steps feel so light I think we might dance, but we don't. After walking to the Quay and looking at the boats and the river, we make our way back to the car and then drive home to Aldeburgh. We say goodbye and I thank Bryony for a lovely time.

"By the way," I say, "you look very beautiful in your flowery dress and your lavender cardigan."

"Thank you," she says, and she drives off, waving.

I walk up the garden path and let myself into an empty house.

CHAPTER FIFTEEN

I am buying a postcard to send to Bryony to say 'thank you'. I have chosen one of the beach at Aldeburgh with a traditional wooden fishing boat sitting on the shingle, white painted sides and an orange gunnel. Almost no one fishes from these beautiful wooden clinker-built boats anymore. It's all GRP (I think that means glass-reinforced plastic), fibre-glass, lightweight and extremely strong, but not beautiful. Not at all. It's as if there is no longer any virtue in beauty. Actually, that's not altogether true. I'm just being grumpy. Some of the modern sailing boats I have seen on the river, and whose hulls are now nearly all fibreglass, are very beautiful. But not the GRP fishing boats on Aldeburgh beach. They are functional, but ugly.

I'm a bit melancholy today. Can't quite say why, just am. It happens to me – out of nowhere I feel sad, deeply sad. I think it might be part of having to be old. Regret. Foreboding. Death. Ceasing to be. Or, perhaps I have memories of a past that William cannot write down. Or hasn't. Leaving me in a kind of limbo. This is an odd thing, an odd part of our relationship. I am shaped by William. That is so. And he has chosen not to give me a past. That is so, too. And yet, sometimes, I have a sense of recollection, as if I can…what is it…remember?

You know I told you I had been reading the poetry of T S Eliot? Well, at the beginning of a poem called *Burnt Norton*, in the very first lines, he says:

> *Time present and time past*
> *Are both perhaps present in time future,*

and then,

> *What might have been and what has been*
> *Point to one end, which is always present.*

Like me. Always present. Mostly, I don't dwell on such things, but today, I'm melancholy, so I do. William is still in London and so my energies are a bit low, and I am on my own, apart from Tabatha. I must do something to cheer myself up.

The trouble is that with William away, I am a bit limited in what I can do. I think my trip to Orford with Bryony was the last thing he wrote, and now that he has other things on his mind, I am, once again, left to moulder. Perhaps that's why I'm down. I can't capture the freedom of my spirit. I'm empty, caught in a time without ending. There's that thing about time again. Is William worrying about his ending? I think so, and maybe that is something else he wants from me. But if he thinks he can just 'kill me off' when he feels like it, watch me suffer to exorcise his own fears, he will find he is mistaken. I have plans!

Anyway, today I can wander about the house or walk down to the Post Office to post my card, but not much else.

I'm at a bit of a loss, but not entirely so. I have my tapestry. William bought it for me – who knows why – I think it was one of those spur of the moment things, and when I am on my own I work the stitches over the painted pattern of the canvas. Red, blue, orange, green, yellow and white. The stitches slant upwards from left to right, a basic half cross-stitch, which, it says on the instructions, is 'a simple form of tent stitch'. I wonder why it's called that. Anyway here I go. Take a deep breath – in and out, through from the back, up and slanting to the right, then down straight and through from the back again. A row of colour, a small patch of colour. Right to left and then left to right. A stitch at a time.

This is what I think: there is much to be gained in these moments alone. Solitude. Loneliness hurts, but there is a dignity to solitude. The practice of solitude. The *deliberate* practice of solitude. Sitting with it. Feeling it. Really feeling what it is like. Attending to it, but letting it be. Surrendering to solitude and a kind of sadness. A stitch at a time.

And now there is Bryony.

CHAPTER SIXTEEN

Despite the stitching, the melancholy persists and I haven't seen Bryony for a while, although I have a feeling that William may be planning something for me. Now that he is back from London, he seems unusually attentive to how I am, asking me if I feel like going out again. Well, I don't. I actually feel like pulling down the window blinds and doing some more mouldering. It's all very well going out and visiting people, but I feel a growing weariness and a wish to be left alone. What may seem to be grumpiness is simply a deliberate determination not to join in. Is there something wrong with that? Most of us spend our lives 'joining in', doing what's required of us, what's expected of us, but sometimes that seems futile, and that is where I am today.

I wake in the mornings on my own. The house is quiet. And as William is not here, I have the house to myself. I walk through from my bedroom into the kitchen and put the kettle on the Aga, putting a tea bag in the small brown teapot and taking from the cupboard my morning tea mug. Although the morning has come, I leave the window blinds pulled down as I take my tea back to my bed, puffing up my pillows and sitting up in bed. I just sit there. Sometimes I read, and sometimes I imagine Tabatha coming onto the bed and curling up at my feet, beginning her morning sleep – which, by the way, continues, on and off, until after lunch. When I get up she does, too, finding the next place to sleep. Then there is breakfast, which I like. I take my time and go at my pace, which is slow. I am content. At peace. The silence and the stillness gather around me. Ah! I can feel it now.

The same happens at night-time. Sleeping by myself as I do, going to bed is full of quietness. Again there is, of course, a ritual, an order to things. First, I pour myself a glass of water and take it with me and put it beside my bed. After changing into my pyjamas, washing my face and cleaning my teeth, I get into bed and read. William has many books, shelf upon shelf, and my favourites are detective stories of all kinds, especially the ones about Inspector Montalbano, which are based in Sicily and are written by Andrea Camilleri. Otherwise, I have an on-going relationship with Proust, whose writing I adore – all those very long sentences. Although I wake in the night at about three in the morning and again at six, I go to sleep easily. I put down my book, turn off my light, settle my pillows and turn onto my right side. Soon I am asleep.

And today, I don't need anyone else, their presence would be a complication, an irritation. Leave me alone.

This morning the phone rang, and as I was on my own I answered it. It was Bryony.

"Abraham, is that you?"

"Yes! It's me."

"I wonder if you would like to have lunch with me today? I am coming into Aldeburgh with my son, Rufus, and his wife

Dotty. We thought we'd have lunch at the Brudenell, and I wondered if you'd like to join us. We have booked a table for twelve forty-five."

"Okay!" I said. Odd that Bryony should have chosen the same restaurant that I had imagined us having lunch in. Do you remember? So, here I am, walking down the town steps on my way to lunch. It's a lovely Aldeburgh day, sunny but with a cold north-easterly wind. I am wearing my long, blue overcoat, and my grey woollen hat. When I arrive at the Brudenell, Bryony and her son and daughter-in-law are already there. Bryony waves and I walk over to the table. In order that I should not forget their names, I have been repeating them to myself – Rufus and Dotty, Rufus and Dotty. Rufus stands and greets me, offering me his hand which I shake.

I think I see in Bryony's smile a mother who loves showing off her son, as she now looks up at him standing there. Why not? He is tall and good-looking. Lanky and bony, with long black hair. Very black. Very long. By contrast, Dotty is petite and blonde. Can she be a dancer, too?

I take my seat opposite Rufus and next to Dotty. Just as I had imagined before, Bryony is facing north and I am facing south. Just a coincidence, I suppose. I listen to Rufus and Dotty talk about their lives. Dotty is not a dancer. They are both teachers, working in a secondary school in the East End of London. Rufus teaches sciences and Dotty history. He talks a lot about the shortage of staff and funding, and about the remarkable resilience and determination of many of their pupils. Not all, though. Some have become completely demoralised with school and cannot wait to leave. They can be troublesome, even sometimes violent. The school is a mix of races and religions, different cultures. For some of the young people there is resentment and anger. It's tough work, but both Rufus and Dotty are dedicated to it. Rufus does most of the talking. Dotty is quieter, and I sense her watching to see how I respond to what is being said.

Our lunch arrives, but just as we are about to start, there is a noise from Bryony's phone, which I now see is lying beside her on the table. Ping! She looks down and there is a picture of someone smiling and waving.

"Excuse me," says Bryony. "It's Veronica. She's just come back from New York. I'll tell her I'll call later." And she sends back a message to her daughter with a face making a kiss. Veronica pings back a 'Thank you' with more kisses. I have never seen this before and am fascinated. Such wonderful immediacy. It's magic, and Bryony's phone is slim, light grey and beautiful. I don't have a phone. I suppose William has not thought it necessary. But now, out of nowhere, I have a vital need to be able to send messages with pictures.

"You must have a phone," says Dotty and produces from her handbag a slim, dusty pink version of Bryony's phone and waves it at me. "How else will you keep in touch?" she says.

How else, indeed. How will I keep 'in touch'?

"I text all the time," says Bryony, "especially with Dotty and Veronica, and sometimes Rufus, although he is often a bit grumpy and less fun to talk to."

"I'm not grumpy!" says Rufus in a grumpy voice.

We all laugh.

We order desserts. Ice cream with chocolate sauce for Rufus and Dotty, and apple and blackberry crumble for both Bryony and me. I like her choice being the same as mine. I know that's silly, but there we are. A kind of intimacy.

But then as the conversation continues, and as Bryony and Rufus share jokes that are familiar to them and even to Dotty, I realise something. They are family, and I am not.

Worse than this, I have no family, or at least not one I know of. I feel rather excluded.

What is happening here? Then I get it. As Dotty and Rufus are looking at something on Dotty's phone, absorbed, I lean towards Bryony and speak softly.

"I have just noticed something about you."

"You have?" she replies.

"I have noticed that you are part of something I cannot know. Something that happened in the past, but which is still here with you now."

"What do you mean?"

"Your life with a much loved husband and with your children. You know all about that, don't you? You can remember it – you have a past."

"Yes, of course."

Rufus and Dotty are now listening.

"Well, as I've told you before, I know nothing about my past. William has never mentioned it, and I don't think he will. He's just made me elderly, living with him here in Suffolk. Apart from what I wear, he has told me almost nothing about myself. I think that's odd."

"Why don't you ask him about it?" says Bryony. "Ever since he first started writing about me, I have always known about my past life."

There is a pause in our conversation. I feel cheated. How unfair that Bryony knows about her past and I know nothing of mine. I know that I come from a place with no past or future, but that part of me which is shaped by William, that part of me I now have to inhabit, has no past. Not yet.

Lunch comes to an end, Bryony insisting on paying the bill, saying that it is her treat, and I walk with them to their car which is parked in the High Street.

"Thank you so much for a lovely lunch," I say. "It was good to meet you Rufus and Dotty. And thank you for showing me your phone, Dotty. I do hope we shall get together again."

As Rufus and Dotty get into the car, Bryony gives me a hug.

"I want to know more about you, Abraham. You must ask William to write something."

"Well, I could," I say, "but I won't. His version would be too ordinary, or even distressing. I could do it for myself, though. So, I shan't mention it to him, I'll just imagine it. And when I have, I'll share it with you."

Bryony smiles.

"I like it when you let your imagination run," she says, and we laugh. Could she know my fantasies? I hope not.

I wave goodbye and walk home, up the town steps counting them as I always do. Forty-six.

William arrives home that evening, not late, about six-fifteen. He looks tired and goes straight into his dressing room to change out of his London clothes and put on something more comfortable: soft trousers, a T-shirt and a blue cashmere cardigan. I am sitting in the garden room with my tapestry. He walks through from the living room and into his study, waving and saying no more than, "Good evening, Abraham."

I wait. I have imagined Tabatha and she is curled up on one of the armchairs close by me. She does no more than twitch an ear when William walks back into the room and sits in the armchair.

"Have you had a good day?" he asks.

"I have, thank you. Bryony took me to lunch at the Brudenell and introduced me to her son and daughter-in-law, who I liked very much. We talked about their work."

"Good, that's good."

"Yes it is, but it made me realise something."

"Oh, yes? And what was that?"

"It made me realise that you have not provided me with a past. You have just brought me here as an old man, without any memories of his past, his family, his childhood. Don't you think that is a bit odd?"

William looks at me as he does sometimes. Not sure quite what to make of me. Someone he has imagined cross-examining him. It's as if he thinks this is not fair. Now I can feel myself getting cross, as if I have been badly treated.

"Don't you think its odd?" I say, again.

William takes in a deep breath and then lets it go.

"I've never thought about it. To be honest, I've never thought about it at all."

Whenever people say, 'to be honest', you know they are going to lie to you. Isn't that right? Well, it was now.

"I simply don't believe you," I say.

Now he is defensive.

"You can believe it or not, but I haven't."

And now he doesn't want to talk about it. I let it go.

"Oh, and by the way, there is something I need, William."

"And that is?"

"I need one of those phones that Bryony and Dotty have."

"An iPhone?"

"I suppose so, if that is what it is called."

"You mean like this?" he says, taking from his pocket a rather battered version of Bryony's phone. It's wrapped in some kind of rubber case.

"Yes, that's it. One of those. I need to keep in touch."

"I see," says William in a rather parental voice.

There is a silence. Is this his chance to make amends?

"Okay," he says, "I'm not sure I like this, but if that's what you want, I'll sort it out."

CHAPTER SEVENTEEN

William has asked me to come into his study to look at the pictures of the latest iPhones on his computer.

"Look at this, Abraham," he says. "My god, it's beautiful! Apparently, it says 'hello to the future'. And it is engineered to resist water and dust. That is very cool."

"Can it send pictures?"

"Oh, yes, it most certainly can."

"So, what happens next?"

"Well, I have to speak to my phone network company. I think I can add you to my contract. And while we're about it, I am going to upgrade my phone, too."

I thought he would.

"I'll deal with it today."

"Okay. Thank you."

I've touched something. I've made a suggestion. Changed the story. And I think this is worrying William. I think he is worrying where it might lead. Will he lose control?

CHAPTER EIGHTEEN

I am holding my new iPhone. It is very beautiful and William has given me a lesson on what it does, much of which I have already forgotten. I am about to send my first text to Bryony. Here goes.

Hi Bryony. It's me.

Swoosh! Now wait for the bubble. And there it is! She is texting me back. Ping!

Hi Abraham. So you have your phone. How great is that? Where are you? Take a picture and send it.

I text back.

Hang on a moment.

Swoosh! Now I've got to try and remember how to do this. I think I've got it. I'm taking a picture of the garden room. I'm adding the message. Swoosh!…The bubble. There it is again. Here it comes. Ping!

The garden room! Well done. I'll send you one.

I'm waiting. There's the bubble. Ping! Bryony's kitchen. This is terrific. What next? I'll try a picture of Tabatha. First, I have to imagine her. There on the chair, washing herself. Swoosh! Wait, wait. Here it comes. Ping!

Nice picture of the chair. Was there something special about it?

How odd. It seems that the technology cannot cope with my imagination. It manages William's, but not mine.

That was meant to be a picture of Tabatha sitting on the chair, but it seems that only the chair came through. I think this means that William's imagination is as far as my phone goes. Hey ho!

Swoosh!

And so, we went on for a while. Swoosh! Ping! Swoosh! Ping! My foot, her teapot, my cup of tea, her saucepans. Then we tired of it and I agreed to call her later in the day.

I wake in the middle of the night and can't go back to sleep. For some reason I can't stop thinking about not having a past. I am lying here within this body that William has given me. An old body with no past. And now I'm thinking about it again. I can't stop myself. I can't help it, I still feel deprived and angry. Angry at William for making me old and not providing me with a family and the kind of memories that

Bryony has, memories of a life before. Now I want a past. And if William won't do it for me, I'll do it for myself. Where shall I start? Let's see what I can do.

I need to start with where I was born and what my parents were like. Let's try this. I was born in Tiptree, just across the border in Essex. My mother's father was a tailor in the East End of London. Some of my father's family were poor farm workers, others were maids and gardeners, servants in other people's houses. There was a large house called High Hall. Perhaps that was where my grandmother was in service. Yes, I think this is right. Then one day she went to a dance in Tiptree and met my grandfather who was, it seems, 'unreliable'. He was working as a porter in what was then the newly opened Wilkins jam factory in Tiptree, but only when he could be bothered to work. There was a roving, tinkerish blood in his veins. He passed this on to my father, Frederick, known as Freddy, who also worked from time to time at the jam factory, but otherwise was a wastrel.

Enter my mother, Fanny. She met my father whilst on holiday in nearby Mersea with her aunt – her mother's sister, Daisy – and her husband, whose name was Arthur. She was smitten at once, for Freddy was handsome and full of words, and he enchanted her. Unfortunately, his words meant nothing, for in addition to being handsome, Freddy, like his father, was also incapable of telling the truth. And then my mother found she was with child – me. It was wartime and her beloved Freddy disappeared. Her parents in London, pious Baptists that they were, disowned her.

Fortunately, Daisy and Arthur took pity on her. They were childless, and they took Fanny into their house as a daughter and then, when the time came, me as a grandson. They brought me up whilst my mother went to work at the local school as a cleaner and canteen lady. Freddy never reappeared. No, let's change that. He did reappear, and for a while all seemed well, but then, one summer a circus arrived in Mersea. The star of the show was a beautiful young woman in a sequinned costume. An acrobat and trapeze artist, who flew across the top of the tent like an exotic bird. She captured the hearts of half the men in Mersea, and most especially that of my father, who left with the circus. This time he really did not come back. And if he had, Arthur would most certainly have shot him with the shotgun he used for killing rabbits.

I went to the local primary school where one teacher in particular, Rose Martin, took me under her wing, and with her help and support I got a place at the grammar school in Colchester. Each morning, at seven-thirty, I would get the bus to Colchester and each evening I would come back again by bus, getting home after five o'clock in the evening. Tea, with Daisy and Arthur, who I thought were my grandparents, then homework, then supper and then bed. They discovered that I was not completely stupid, and I did well at school. And then...And then what?

Something's happened. It's gone. I can't remember. Is that it? Or is something else happening. Hang on...It's not that I can't remember, it's that *I don't want to remember*. Suddenly, I'm feeling uneasy. It's as if the remembering has upset me. It is as if I was beginning to feel that I couldn't know who I was now without knowing who I had been before. Can you see what I was doing? I was beginning to justify myself; build a picture of myself as someone worthy, worth being. Do you see that? 'I did well at school.' You see, I'd made myself clever. But what if I wasn't clever? What then? And have I been married? Were we happy? And how did it end? STOP! I've opened a box labelled 'Past' and it's bringing me no comfort at all.

I'm not going to do this. Here I am already wondering what I did in my life, who I was. How successful was I? Did people like me? And my wife, did she die or did she leave me? Am I a widower? Loss, loneliness, suffering. You see what I'm doing? I am not going to do this. I've got to stop – forget it. William has given me no past, and perhaps that is a blessing. I am as I am. I am as you find me, as I find myself. Surely that is enough? I regain my freedom.

I have a sudden and desperate need to talk to Bryony, but it is the middle of the night. I doze fitfully until early morning, then I text her.

I need to talk to you urgently.

Swoosh! I wait. Perhaps she's still asleep. Then the bubble appears. Ping!

Whatever's happened?

I text back.

I must talk to you.

She replies. Ping!

Do you want to come and see me? Do you want me to come and collect you?

I reply.

Yes please.

Swoosh!

Okay. I'll be there shortly.

Bryony comes in her car and takes me to her house. Before we go in, we stand for a while on her veranda looking out towards the sea and I feel refreshed by the cool, salty air. The wind is strong from the south-east, sweeping long white-crested waves along the coast from Aldeburgh and crashing them onto the shore. We stand and we look.

"Is this why you stayed here?" I ask.

"Yes, of course," she says. She watches the waves, listening to the sound of the shingle as it is dragged back by the sea. "It was the sea and the tide that held me. When all seemed lost, they gave me a sense of wholeness and continuity, of being a very small part of something magnificent, and this comforted me. It still does. Now I cannot imagine not being here."

"It's a good place to live, Bryony."

We walk into the living room and I sit in one of the arm-chairs. Bryony brings in two mugs of tea, putting them on the low table between us.

"So, what is it that you need to say to me?" she asks.

Now that we are sitting together with our tea, I have forgotten. Oh, yes. My past.

"You know we talked about my not having a past, and I said I would imagine one?"

"Yes, I do. I'm looking forward to hearing about it."

"Well, that's the point. I started to imagine that I remembered my past, but then I had to stop."

"Why?"

"Because I was painting this picture of myself, and I was beginning to want it to be something special. You know, a clever kid, a happy marriage, meaningful work. I was beginning to feel I couldn't *be* without it. But then what if it wasn't like that? What if I wasn't clever, or was unhappily married and just worked to make ends meet? What then? How would I feel about myself? Or what if I just felt inadequate, not good enough, always seeking approval? The more of my past that I 'remembered' the more I began to feel discontented and insecure. I realised that I was beginning to feel trapped by it. And then I thought, hang on, perhaps I am blessed with having no past? If I am just as I am, without a past, perhaps I can just be as I am now. Would you like me any more, or even any less, if you knew who I had been before?"

Bryony looks across at me.

"I like you as you are, Abraham, just knowing you as you are. In fact I like you very much as you are, sitting here and drinking a mug of tea. By the sea."

"Yes, by the sea. Living by the sea."

"So, what are you going to do?"

"Nothing. I'm going to do nothing. It is such a relief. I can be myself."

We look at each other and smile big smiles that then give way to uncontrollable laughter. It is as if we have just discovered something miraculous, although I suspect that Bryony does not yet know what it is. The wonderment of the moment lived without regret or expectation. I am feeling much better. I wonder again whether I should tell Bryony who I really am, but decide against it. Not now.

"And anyway," says Bryony, "as time goes on, you and I will make memories together, won't we?"

"Yes, we will Bryony. Thank you."

"Thank you for what?"

"For liking me as I am."

"You're welcome."
We laugh.

That night back in my bed at William's house, I think about what it is that one day I will have to tell Bryony. That beyond the roles we are given by William, and whatever our 'purpose' is for him, we have a much larger freedom, a freedom of spirit; that no one can own their dæmon, or the characters that they write, only call them up, unsure of how they will be and what they will do. Poor William, I only wish he could share in that freedom. Perhaps that is still to come.

PART THREE

LIVING BY THE SEA

CHAPTER NINETEEN

It is morning. The vivid colours of my dreaming are fading. In the light they slip away as the day takes hold. I am always surprised when I dream at night, which is often. Because I am no more than a fiction, a man without a past, I had supposed that I would not dream, but I do. Dreams of adventure and a kind of wildness. Where do they come from? Last night I dreamt that Bryony and I were voyaging on a wondrous sailing boat. She had taken the helm and I was peering into the distance. I'm not sure what I was looking for. Perhaps nothing very much. Or perhaps it was for land, because all of a sudden the boat had gone and we were naked, swimming in a pool surrounded by trees. And then I was awake, smiling. Tabatha was curled up on my bed.

CHAPTER TWENTY

Today, I have arranged to have lunch with Bryony. I have booked a table for twelve-thirty and agreed to meet Bryony there. I am sitting at the table when Bryony arrives. I wave and she walks over. Beside her is a young woman with short cut black hair and a fringe, a simple T-shirt and frayed jeans. Open sandals on her feet, painted toenails. Black.

"Abraham, this is Veronica, my daughter. I hope you don't mind if she joins us?"

"Not at all. Good to meet you Veronica."

"And it's good to meet you Abraham."

She smiles.

I call over the waitress and explain that we are now three of us, and she sets an extra place. Our table is by the window overlooking the sea. Once again, Bryony sits looking north and I sit looking south. But now Bryony has Veronica by her side, and Veronica is intriguing. There is something in her dark eyes that both keeps you out and invites enquiry. She looks out towards the sea and I follow her gaze. With a strong north-easterly, the waves are high, white topped and tumbling onto the shingle, one after another. As she looks, she smiles, and at once I can see that she is at home beside the sea. Our waitress arrives with menus and offers us water.

"Yes please, I say. And no ice. Is that okay Veronica?"

"Yes, that's fine."

"Do you eat fish? The fish is good here and there's normally a catch of the day."

"Well, actually I'm vegan," she says.

"Okay, let's see what they can do for you."

I call the waitress over and ask her whether they can provide a vegan menu.

"Oh, yes," she says, "we have a vegan menu." She hurries off to bring it to us.

So, we order our food and our wine. I want to know about Veronica, but don't know how to begin. Bryony comes to the rescue.

"Veronica plays the violin," she says. "Amongst other things, she plays with the BBC Symphony Orchestra and with a quartet called Harmonia. The quartet are here in Snape for a concert at the weekend. Veronica has come down a day early to see me. Rehearsals start tomorrow – then there will be no more going out to lunch!"

Veronica laughs.

"Yes, quite right," she says. "We'll be hard at work tomorrow."

"How long have you been playing with the BBC?" I ask.

"It's four years now. I had a lucky break. I was doing some recording work with the woman called Clare, who is the first violin with the orchestra, and she let me know that there was about to be a vacancy. She liked the way I play and got me an audition, and I was accepted. Then a year later, when Clare was putting together her quartet, she asked me to be part of it. Of course, I said yes."

"And what made you want to be a violinist?"

Unexpectedly, Veronica leans across and places her hand on mine. A light touch. "That's like asking me why I breathe," she says.

And I watch as Bryony looks at her daughter with the kind of love I can only imagine.

It's a good lunch, with Veronica telling us what it's like to be part of an orchestra, and the differences in playing as a quartet. She prefers the quartet because there's more freedom to express herself. We drive back to Bryony's house and Veronica says that she has to go to Snape to meet up with her colleagues.

Left alone, Bryony offers me tea. We take our mugs and sit on the veranda looking out over the sea where a ferry from Felixstowe is disappearing over the horizon to the Hook of Holland.

"You must be very proud of your daughter," I say.

"I am, but it's been hard for her. Getting a place with the orchestra was the first lucky break she'd had in some while."

I wait for Bryony to continue, knowing that there is something she wants to tell me. Something about her daughter.

"Veronica is divorced. She'd only been married for three years when she discovered she couldn't have children. It was a great shock to her and to her husband. They'd both wanted children, very much."

Again she paused. Something painful.

"Her husband could not come to terms with it. It destroyed their marriage and he left her, heartbroken. Anyway, she had her music and that became her refuge, but that was hard, too. As you can tell from what Veronica said at lunch, the world of classical music and orchestras is not for the faint-hearted. It's physically demanding, too. Like dancing, I suppose…And for a while, she struggled to get work. Then Providence stepped in and she met Clare, just by chance it seemed. At last her hard work and dedication was rewarded."

Another pause, unsure of whether to go on. Bryony looks out towards the horizon, holding her mug of tea in both hands.

"I'd love to hear her play," I say. "Do you think we could go to the concert at Snape?"

Bryony turns to me and smiles. "Well, Veronica has given me a ticket. Let me see if I can get another. I'll text her and let you know."

For a while, we sit together and say nothing more. Then, just as her daughter had done, Bryony reaches over and touches my hand. But this time she holds my hand in hers.

"It was a lovely lunch, Abraham. Thank you for taking us. I like being with you."

"Me, too. I like being with you, and I liked your daughter. There is a great sadness about her. Something dark. I would like to know her better."

CHAPTER TWENTY-ONE

It is three o'clock in the morning and I am awake. Wide awake. I sit up in bed and switch on the bedside light. I check the clock and take a drink from my glass of water. I am familiar with this time of night. One of the pleasures of William making me old is that I am able to discover the special quality of the time between two and six in the morning. In the teaching of Ayurveda, this is *Vata* time, a time when the realm of the Divine is most present, a time of opening and receptivity. Don't ask me why I know this, I just do. I suppose William must have told me. I pull back the curtains and everything is dark and still. I am thinking about Veronica and hoping that I will be able to hear her play.

Seven o'clock and I am laying out my breakfast. And today it's porridge, made with milk and honey, into which I have cut half of a banana and some dried apricots. Before I eat I pause and close my eyes laying my hands on the table palms down. Breathe in, breathe out. I like to start my day like this. The house is quiet and very still.

I don't know where William is. He has been away for a few days and I am not sure when he is coming back. He doesn't always tell me these things. I think I will go for a walk across the marsh to the river.

Ping! Bryony has sent me a text.

I have tickets for the concert. It starts at seven. Shall I pick you up?

I text back.

That's great. Pick me up at about six. That will give us plenty of time, and we could have a drink before the concert.

I am thinking about a vodka martini.

We are on our way. Bryony has swapped her ticket so that we can sit together. Arriving early, we take our drinks – Bryony chooses a white wine – and sit for a while looking over the marsh towards the river and Iken, with its church in the distance at the water's edge, amongst trees. Then the bell rings and we take our seats towards the back of the concert hall, which is set on a steep rake. The concert begins and the four young women walk onto the stage dressed in black, but each with a coloured flower in her hair. Veronica's is red, blood red. Two violins, a viola and a cello. They bow to us and then sit, tuning their instruments. I look at the programme. Clare is first violin and Veronica is second violin. The viola is played by Rosemary and the cello by Sonia. The programme has a photo of each of them and a short paragraph of 'biography', and I see that all of them with the exception of Veronica trained at the Guildhall School of Music in London. That must be where the others first met.

They begin with a piece by Ravel, lively and bright. The next is by Britten, his Quartet Number Two in C Major. Sombre. There is then a short interlude and we walk out onto the terrace of the concert hall. Another vodka martini for me and a sparkling water for Bryony. We return and the quartet starts again with something bright by a composer I have never heard of. Then they begin a piece by Haydn. I look at the programme. 'Op 64 in D Major'. After the first movement, 'Allegro Moderato', comes the second, 'Adagio e Cantabile'. I am captured. It is so beautiful. And then I feel the tears running down my cheeks. I'm weeping, uncontrollably. Perhaps it's the vodka! I put my hand to my face and Bryony reaches over to me and places her hand on my arm. The movement ends. There is a pause and then the third and final movements, but I don't really hear them. There is applause and a man near to me calls 'Bravo!' I am sitting there, but I'm in some other place. After a while, I realise that only Bryony and I are left. Everyone else has gone. Then Veronica appears by the stage and we stand up and walk down to her.

"So, how was that?" she asks.

"It was lovely," says Bryony, "and Abraham wept when he heard the Adagio."

Veronica looks at me and then from out of nowhere, she throws her arms around me and holds me.

"I am going to like you," she says.

I smile. "That would be nice."

"Yes it would," she says.

At that moment Clare walks towards us and Veronica introduces her. She has very short cropped blonde hair with light blue eyes. I shake her hand, which is slim with long, beautiful fingers. The hand of an excellent violinist. I say how much I enjoyed the concert.

"He wept in the Adagio," says Veronica, and they smile at each other as if this was to be expected.

When Bryony and I get back to her house, we sit on the veranda and listen to the sea. I am still somehow caught in the music we have just heard and in the gentle dignity of Veronica and her companions. For some while we just sit there. Then Bryony walks into the house to get a shawl to wrap around her shoulders. She brings one for me.

"This is such a good place to be," she says.

"Yes, it is."

At that moment a sudden and irrepressible thought comes to me.

"Bryony," I say, "would it be possible for me to stay in your Guest House for a few days?"

"Why yes, of course. When would you like to come?"

"Tomorrow?"

"Okay, tomorrow. Shall I drive you home?"

As we drive back along the coast road, I find myself thinking about the concert, and then I realise what I am doing. I am remembering. Somewhere inside me, I am taken back. I can hear the music, see the quartet, remember when Veronica held me in her arms. It's all there. I have a store-cupboard with memories in it, a past. A wonderful store-cupboard. I see it. It is made of washed oak, painted with flowers and vine leaves.

And tomorrow I shall stay in the Guest House. I must order a taxi.

The following morning, at about ten-thirty, the Squirrel Taxi takes me to Sandy Bar. I ordered it on William's account. I'm sure he won't mind. He drops me outside Bryony's house and carrying my overnight bag, I walk round to the front and see her walking up from the sea, arms folded across her chest, her head bowed. She looks up, sees me and waves. I wave back.

"I'll get the key." She takes from a hook by the front door, a key with a label: 'Guest House'.

"Follow me."

And I do.

Bryony unlocks the door. It opens into a room with a bed and a comfy looking armchair. A colourful rug on the floor. At the back of the room is another door that leads into a bathroom. The bed, a double, has been made up with grey linen pillows and a matching duvet. There is a small table with an electric kettle. It's perfect.

"I hope you'll be comfortable," she says. "There's an electric radiator if you are cold. I've never slept here, but I'm told it is very snug. Settle in. I'll be next door."

She walks out leaving the front door open. I sit on the bed and listen. I can hear the sea. I put my pyjamas under the duvet and my wash bag in the bathroom. I can't really believe I'm here and I wonder what William will think when he gets home. I left him a note.

Two days have passed and this morning Bryony dropped me off at William's house to pick up some clothes I had forgotten.

She will pick me up later. When I come into the house, I find William sitting in his study, so I walk through to see him.

He looks up from his computer and turns his desk chair around towards me.

"Ah, Abraham, good to see you. How are you getting on in the Guest House?"

"I'm fine. I wake to the sound of the sea."

"And Bryony, is she content to have you as her guest?"

"Seems to be, for the moment. Were you surprised?"

"I was a bit, but I'm glad you have someone you want to be with, and glad that you seem to enjoy each other's company. What did you make of Veronica?"

"I think she's lovely."

"She's a wonderful violinist."

"Yes, she is."

"To be part of the BBC Symphony Orchestra is a considerable achievement."

"Yes, I can imagine it is."

William turns back to his computer.

"By the way, I'm just here to pick up some more clothes. If it's okay with you I shall stay at the Guest House for the time being."

"Yes, that's fine. Do you want me to run you back?"

"No, it's okay. Bryony is going to pick me up in about an hour."

I walk through to my bedroom where Tabatha is lying curled up on my bed. She looks up when I walk in.

"And where have you been?" she says.

"I've been staying with Bryony at her house in Thorpeness."

"Very nice for you."

"You seem cross."

"Well, it leaves me a bit in the lurch, doesn't it?"

"I suppose it does. I hadn't thought about it."

"No, you wouldn't have, would you?"

I lean over to stroke her head, but she growls and strikes out at me with her paw.

"What's that all about?"

"You just don't get it, do you? You think you can imagine me as and when you like and otherwise just forget I'm here."

"But you're not 'here'. You're just part of my imagination."

"Oh, so that's alright is it? Just part of your wretched imagination. Oh, lucky old me. That's fine is it?"

I sit on the bed, and Tabatha sits up and starts cleaning herself, licking her leg with her long, pink tongue.

"Don't worry about me, I'll be fine," she says between licks.

I go to the chest of drawers and take out clean underwear and some shirts. Three pairs of socks and five handkerchiefs. I open my cupboard and take out another pair of black cords and a woollen cardigan with a roll collar.

I put all of the clothes in my overnight bag. Tabatha sits looking at me. Then I have an idea.

"How would you like to live by the sea?" I ask.

Tabatha stands and walks across the bed.

"I thought you would never ask," she says.

And so I open my bag and she settles into it.

As we are driving back to Bryony's house, I have my bag on my lap and Tabatha pushes her head out.

"Oh my God, you've brought Tabatha!"

She can see her!

"Do you mind?" I ask.

"Not at all. She is beautiful."

Tabatha begins to purr.

As soon as we walk into the house Tabatha steps out of my bag and stretches. She walks up to Bryony and rubs her head against her leg. I get growled at and Bryony gets immediate affection. What's that about? Tabatha walks around the room, finds one of the armchairs and jumps up onto it. She then curls up and goes to sleep. Bryony looks at me and smiles.

"I'll just go and put these things in the Guest Room," I say.

"Okay. I have to go to Waitrose to get some food. Do you want to come?"

"I'll come."

I hope you are paying attention, William. This is how love begins.

CHAPTER TWENTY-TWO

I am having breakfast with Bryony. She is quiet. She seems to be turning something over in her mind. In the weeks that I have come to know her, I've seen this before. She will go quiet, turn into herself, and then, sometime later, say whatever it is she has been thinking about. I sit beside her and let her be. I'm thinking about what I might do for the rest of the day. Not much. I am about to go back to the Guest House when Bryony asks me to stay for a while with her.

"The weekend after next is Christmas," she says, "and Veronica has asked if she can come and stay with me and bring a friend with her. His name is Alex."

"Which is good?"

"Yes, which is good. But they'll need the Guest House."

"Yes, of course. Of course. I can move out."

"Or…"

"Or what?"

"You could stay with me."

"Stay with you?"

"Yes, stay with me."

"You mean sleep on your sofa?"

"Well, you could do that. It is comfortable. Or you could sleep in my attic room. It has a rather small single bed. Or you could sleep with me. I have a large bed."

"You think we could do that?"

"We could try."

"Okay. If you say so."

"I do."

We look at each other and then laugh.

"We'll try it out, see if it works," she says.

"Okay."

You see what happens?

It is now eight days since Bryony and I decided to try sleeping together, and we like it. We haven't slept together every night, but when we have, we have gone to bed at about nine-fifteen, which gives us time to read before we put out the light. In the morning we come close together and talk about what we have dreamt or what we might do in the day. We are tender, but our love-making when it happens is quite unlike the panting love-making of the young or anything you can read about in books. Gentle touching, lying close together, holding each other. We like it. And then we have had days when we have slept apart.

So, now we are ready for Christmas!

It is Christmas Eve and we are waiting for Veronica and Alex to arrive. Bryony has decorated her living room with a small tree with baubles and Christmas lights, and she has strung white lights along the eaves of her veranda. Tabatha and I are sitting together in one of the armchairs of Bryony's living room. Tabatha seems to have forgiven me. I am feeling festive.

A moment ago, Bryony's phone went Ping! It was Veronica to say they were two minutes away, and now they are here. They come onto the veranda with their bags, and I note that Veronica has brought her violin with her. Bryony takes them to the Guest House, making sure they have everything they need. They come back and Bryony goes into the kitchen to make some tea while Veronica flops down onto the sofa, tired by their journey, and Alex takes one of the armchairs. He is tall, lanky, bony, with shocking red hair cut short at the sides and long on top. Loose fitting sweatshirt and jeans.

"We're so pleased to be here," says Veronica. "London has been chaotic over the last few days, and we've had one rehearsal after another. We're exhausted."

I am assuming that Alex must also be a musician. Tall enough to play the double bass!

"How was the drive?"

"Pretty awful. I suppose that there are lots of people doing what we're doing. Going home for Christmas. Wasn't that the name of a movie? Something like that."

We have tea and listen to Veronica and Alex talking about their latest concerts. As I had guessed, Alex is a musician, and he also plays with the BBC Symphony Orchestra. But not the double bass. Saxophone and clarinet. It turns out later that Alex also brought his clarinet, but he has left it in the boot of the car, too embarrassed to bring it in. I like that. Veronica is telling us about a European tour being planned for the Harmonia Quartet in the New Year. We have tea and chocolate biscuits, the ones that taste of ginger. We are content.

Christmas morning. I wake early and at six o'clock I am sitting in my pyjamas in an armchair with Tabatha, looking out into the darkness. Then I see a light along the shore-line. Someone is walking with a torch. I get up, and putting on my coat, hat and shoes, I walk across the dune to the beach. It's Veronica. Hearing my steps on the shingle, she turns.

"Can't sleep?"

"I always wake early," she says. "Usually before six, and as soon as I wake, I hear music. I'm very sensitive to sounds. I hear them through my fingers, like the vibration of a violin string. And today I heard the sea and was drawn to it."

We look out over the water and now, I too hear the sound of the waves turning gently onto the sand and pebbles. Veronica switches off her torch. The darkness gathers us in.

"I am ridiculously sensitive to all kinds of vibration," she says, "including the vibration of people. Do you feel it?"

"No, I don't think I do. Sometimes I can sense how someone is feeling, but I'm not sure that I feel it as a vibration."

"For me it is a physical sensation and at times it can be difficult to bear. Here, especially, I feel Mum's lingering feeling of loss. Her deep sadness. Mine, too, of course. I was very close to my father you know, and I still grieve for him. When I am with my mother, it becomes more intense. That's when I have to find a separate place to be. To recover my self."

We walk a little way along the beach.

"Did you know that I live in what was my parents' house in London?"

"No, I didn't know that."

"When Dad died and Mum decided to stay here, I asked if I could live in the London house. I was looking for a place to live, and it's a lovely Edwardian terraced house in Battersea, just off the Northcote Road. It's a bit big for me on my own, but anyway Mum said yes, so I moved in. Of course, she may decide one day to move back."

"Yes, I suppose so, but she seems very content living by the sea doesn't she?"

"Yes, she does. And perhaps you're right. Perhaps she will always want to live here."

We walk back and Veronica goes into the Guest House. In these short moments I have found how different Veronica is from her mother. Bryony is bright, outgoing, hopeful, I think. Despite having touched my hand at lunch and then embraced me at the concert, Veronica is by nature much more withdrawn, reaching into herself for the strength that her mother takes from whatever is around her. And she feels vibrations. I want to know more. If both William's and my destiny lie in what we may find in Bryony, I have a sense that mine may also be shaped by the world inhabited by her daughter. Oh, and by the way, she can see Tabatha, too.

Christmas Day begins with a clear sky, the sun rising from below the eastern horizon just after eight o'clock. At about eight-thirty Bryony walks into the living room in her dressing gown. She strokes Tabatha on her head and comes to sit beside me, taking my arm.

"Happy Christmas, Abraham!"

I lift her hand and kiss it.

"Happy Christmas, Bryony! Thank you for having me here today."

It was a lovely Christmas Day. A walk along the beach to Aldeburgh and back. Lunch with all the trimmings and apple crumble. None of us wanted Christmas pudding, but we did have mince pies and brandy butter. Then we persuaded Veronica and Alex to play us Christmas music, including some carols that we could sing.

Bryony was given a very special present. Veronica, Rufus and Dotty had got together and bought her a laptop computer. An Apple MacBook. I know, it sounds impossible, but Veronica said they had decided that it was time that Bryony began exploring beyond herself, and the laptop would offer her all sorts of ways of looking things up on the web. They said it would open up another world to her. She has spent much of the day 'searching'.

In the evening we played Scrabble and talked, and Bryony produced a jigsaw puzzle and a special board on which we could lay it out. The puzzle had a picture of Father Christmas flying through the air above the roof tops, in one thousand pieces. For the first time I felt what it might be like to be part of a family. I kept this to myself.

Veronica and Alex stayed until the morning after Boxing Day, and then they drove back to London. I returned to the Guest House. At New Year, Bryony and I had supper together and then walked along the shingle to watch the fireworks organised on the beach by the Thorpeness Country Club. There was quite a crowd.

"We shall remember this," said Bryony.

Remembering. More for my store-cupboard.

CHAPTER TWENTY-THREE

William has called me on my iPhone. He is going to be away for a month and wants me to house-sit for him. There was a time when such a long separation would have been difficult for me to manage. My energy levels would have dropped so low that I would have had to shut myself away in the house and wait. But something had changed. Day by day, I had begun to feel more independent, literally less dependent, and now, even though I would rather stay with Bryony, I know that I shall be fine.

"It's just that a month is quite a long time to leave the house empty," he says.

But this can hardly be the point. He has been away before and never worried about leaving his house empty, although even if I'm here I'm not sure what I would do if anything happened, like a burst pipe or a blocked drain. Then I see it. This is not about his house. It is about me and Bryony. I think he is jealous. Having put me on the page to explore his own anxieties and despair, his fear of getting old and being unloved and unloving, and then seeing me making my friendship with Bryony, he thinks I have abandoned him. So, now he's trying to draw me back, away from Bryony. It is such foolishness. If only he could open his eyes! But of course, he can't. Although he is writing both of us, Bryony and me, he cannot yet see what is happening, really happening. He cannot see that he and I should be sharing a path. Can you see that? Maybe not. Not yet.

"Do you really think this is necessary?" I say.

"Of course I do. I wouldn't ask if I thought it wasn't."

"Well, why this sudden concern for the security of your house? You've never mentioned it before."

There is silence at the other end of the phone. When he speaks he is angry.

"Listen, Abraham, get this into your head. It is not for you to tell me what I should or should not do. That is not how it works."

"But it's alright for you to tell me what to do, is it?"

"Yes, of course it is," he says, his voice rising. "And just remember, you are nothing without me."

If only you knew William. If only you knew. If only you would let Bryony and me write the story for you; bring the words to the page for you. Let go and receive. And now I am cross.

I press the red 'Off' button, put down my phone and walk out onto the veranda. I breathe deeply and taste the salt in the air, hear the squawking of the herring gulls. They are always there, or black-headed gulls and occasionally a large black-backed gull swooping down low, searching the shallow waters close to the shore. I walk down to the water's edge and pick up a handful of pebbles. One at a time, I throw them into the waves.

Then I walk back to the house, pick up my phone and call William.

"Okay. I'll house-sit for you. Pick me up tomorrow morning."

I find Bryony in the kitchen, and I tell her what William has asked for, or rather what he has commanded.

"Oh, my darling Abraham," she says. "I am so sorry." She takes me in her arms and holds me close. "Why is William doing this?"

"I'm not sure," I say, "but it's not about looking after his house."

That night we sleep together.

So, here I am, back in William's house, which feels empty. I decided to leave Tabatha with Bryony. Although I no longer mind being on my own, without the sea and the shingle, I feel at a loss. I was living by the sea for just over a month, and had settled in, become used to it. The expanse of sky, the constant sighing of the waves, the crying of the gulls. The Guest House, Bryony, Christmas, Veronica and Alex, the beach and the sea. And now I am sitting in the garden room and remembering them. I don't know whether Bryony will want me to come back when William returns. I think so. But anyway, for the moment I am here, and with William away, I may be rather stuck in one place, or that is what I am supposing. We shall see.

Getting to know Bryony, of whom I am very fond, becoming close to her and in some way becoming part of her life, including her children, has enriched my sense of being Abraham Soar. And although I come from a different place, we are kin. I guess that if we are to bring William to the place he seeks, we will have to be patient. And determined.

So, do you see how it is for me? How I have to be both part fiction and part storyteller. Part of me is constrained and shaped by William, and part of me is free. Free to adventure and to love. This is the life of the dæmon spirit! Especially the loving and being loved. And now that I, Abraham Soar, have memories, something in my store-cupboard, everything has changed. When I am with William I still feel his fear, his isolation, but when I am with Bryony, and when I am by the sea, I feel utterly connected with love.

So…here's the thing. What to do? There is fear and there is love. What will I, Abraham Soar, do?

I have the answer. I shall choose love. Indeed, I intend to cultivate love, for myself, for Bryony and for William – not that he will notice! Well, not yet. I am content and ready for whatever might come. This morning I shall walk across the marshes to the river.

Evening. I am sitting in the garden room when my mobile goes Ping! It is Bryony.

Abraham, can you come to me? I need rescuing. Bring an overnight bag.

I text back.

Of course. I'll be over straight away.

I put a few things in my bag, order a taxi and go to Bryony's house. It is dark, but the light on the veranda is on. I knock on the door and Bryony opens it. She has been crying. I walk in and Bryony asks me to sit with her on the sofa.

114

"What's happened?" I ask, putting my arms around her.

"Most of the time, I manage," she says, "but every so often a chasm opens and I begin to fall in. The loss, the being left behind. It's enormous. Today is the third anniversary of Jonathan's death. It has been more than I can bear."

"I am so sorry. I had no idea."

"It's okay. How could you have known? And I thought I was doing fine until suddenly I wasn't. Thank you for coming."

"Of course I would come."

For a long while we just sit together. From time to time the crying returns, but then it begins to subside.

"Can we go to bed?" she asks.

"Yes, I should like that."

We go to bed and we curl into each other. I hold her in my arms until she falls asleep. Gently, I remove my arm from around her and lie on my back in the silence.

I must have gone to sleep, too, because now I am awake and Bryony is standing beside me with two mugs of tea. She has drawn back the curtains and the sun is shining.

"Good morning, Abraham."

"Good morning, Bryony. Are you okay?"

"Yes, I'm much better this morning. Thank you for rescuing me."

"My pleasure."

We sit up in bed and drink our tea.

"What time is it?" I ask.

"Nearly nine-thirty."

"I can't believe we slept that long."

"Well, we did, or at least you did. I've been up since about eight. Shall we treat ourselves to chocolate in Orford?"

"Well, that would be lovely."

And so we get up and shower and dress.

It is now afternoon. We had a great drive to Orford, once again having chocolate and croissants at the Pump House Bakery and then walking down to the Quay and back. I know, repetition. It was one of those bright, sunny and cold Suffolk days, with a light south-easterly wind. We were well wrapped up and by the time we got back to Bryony's house we felt refreshed. We are now sitting on the veranda, still in our coats and scarves.

"Veronica is coming to stay for a couple of nights, driving down tomorrow morning. She wants to stay in the attic room. By herself. Would you come and have lunch with us? I guess you have to go back to William's house tonight, but I could ask Veronica to pick you up on her way."

"Okay, I should like that. I hope Veronica won't mind picking me up."

"Of course not. She's already told me that she's becoming rather fond of you. When she lost her father, it hit her very hard, and I think she talks to you in the same sort of way she talked to him."

Veronica arrives at William's house just after midday and I am ready for her. She gives me a hug and I get into her very small car. We drive off towards Sandy Bar.

"How was the journey?"

"Not bad. A lot of lorries on the A12. And how are you?"

"I'm okay. A bit bored at having to house-sit for William."

"Oh, is that what you are doing? I was wondering why you were here and not with Mum. By the way, I have something I want to talk to you about."

"Okay."

"It's a book I have been reading. I'll tell you about it after lunch. If you can stay."

"Yes, I can stay."

We arrive and Bryony is there to greet us, smiling, her hair more wild than usual. We have lunch and then Bryony takes the plates off the table and walks into the kitchen, before returning and sitting beside us on the sofa. Veronica opens her handbag and takes out a book. She is centre stage, and Bryony watches her.

"I want to read you something from the book I told you about. It's called *Unbinding* and it is written by Kathleen Dowling Singh. Actually, I should say 'was written', since she died shortly after the book was published. Anyway, it's a kind of commentary on the Buddhist teachings of suffering and how things come to be. It's wonderful, and this is what I want to read to you."

She opens the book and finds the right page.

"These are the opening paragraphs of a chapter titled 'It's Hard to Be a Person'."

"Good title."

"Yes. Now listen, this is how it starts:

It's hard to be a person. We all know that. Rarely, though, do we fully share such a disclosure with each other.
That's true isn't it? We rarely share how difficult it is to be who we are."

117

I say, "I guess that's so." Bryony nods and smiles in agreement. Veronica continues. "So, then she says:

We isolate ourselves, believing that the unease we feel is normal or that no one else feels it or that everyone else feels it and they just have better masks.

Now, here's the point:

This thinking keeps each of us feeling even more separate, isolated in silent discouragement or shame. We forget that honest self-disclosure keeps us in communion with each other."

Veronica puts down the book and we sit in the silence the words have created. Then Bryony sits down beside Veronica and takes her hand. She doesn't say anything, there is no need, and after a while Veronica stands up and stretches.

"I think I'll take my things up to my room, Mum."

I get up and sit beside Bryony on the sofa. Left by ourselves, we continue to sit quietly for a while.

"Honest self-disclosure," says Bryony, looking across at me. "I like that. It makes me think about all that you and I shared yesterday. I suppose that was honest disclosure. And wasn't it true that it brought us into some kind of communion?"

"Yes," I say, "I think it did."

"But then this morning," she says, "I was thinking something else. Something else about sharing who we are. I was thinking that with you, Abraham, pretty much what I see is what there is. Pretty much it's who you are. No past. No hidden secrets. At least none that I know of! It's very unusual, but it makes you easy to be with."

"That's good."

"Yes, it is."

And Bryony leans against me resting her head on my shoulder. We sit like this, watching the seagulls sweep over the waves in the fading light.

"When does William come back?"

"In about two weeks."

"Will you come back to the Guest House?"

"Yes, I should like that. I miss the sea. And Tabatha."

"And me a bit, I hope."

"Yes, of course, you too Bryony. And we have work to do."

Bryony drives me back to William's house.

"There is a sadness in Veronica isn't there?" I say.

"Yes. A deep sadness."

CHAPTER TWENTY-FOUR

William is back. He arrived this morning. He looks tired and has hardly spoken to me. He just said "Hello" and went straight into his study, where he is now. I am making him some tea. I have put the small brown pot on a tray with a cup and two McVitie's Digestive biscuits, which I know he likes. I walk through the living room and into his study.

"I thought you might like some tea."

"Thank you, Abraham. That's most kind. Sorry to be a bit distracted, but I had something I had to send off, and now I'm catching up on emails."

I place the tray on his worktop.

"Was everything okay while I was away?"

"Yes, pretty much."

I don't mention Bryony's distress, or Veronica's visit, although I assume he knows these things. Perhaps he doesn't.

"And how was your trip?"

"It was good. I had to spend the first ten days in London attending various meetings and stuff, and then I took the train to Devon to take part in a two-week residential course at Schumacher College in Dartington. It was called 'Harmony, Ecology and Education'."

"What was that all about?"

"Well, the first few days were organised by Richard Brown. I've probably told you about him before."

"I don't think so."

"He is the headmaster of a primary school in Sevenoaks in Kent, and for some years now he has been bringing principles of Harmony into the school curriculum. It's fascinating. They have even converted part of the school playing field into a vegetable garden and orchard, and they grow some of their own food. Each week one class of children takes responsibility for monitoring and measuring the food waste, which is then put into their compost bins and, eventually, back on to the vegetable beds."

"That sounds good."

"It is, and Richard Brown is inspirational. Quite a number of the people on the course were teachers or young people going into teaching. Then – and this was wonderful – a man from the Prince's School of Traditional Arts in London, whose patron is The Prince of Wales, gave us a three-day introduction into Sacred Geometry."

"What's that?"

"You would have loved it."

"I would?"

"Yes, I think you would. It was all about the geometric patterns and forms that we see in Nature, and how these forms and proportions are in everything we see, including our own bodies and the cathedrals, temples and mosques of the great faiths. What was good about it was that we actually got to work with compasses and rulers, drawing the patterns that arise from the basic shapes of circles, squares and triangles. One of the most fascinating things he showed us was the orbits of Venus and the Earth around the Sun, which, when drawn, reveal the shape of a beautiful flower based upon pentagrams."

"I'd like to see that."

"I can show you. He gave us this link to a YouTube video. Look." And William opens up a video on his computer and there we see the Earth and Venus orbiting the Sun and the mid-point between them tracing this astonishingly beautiful shape.

"He even had us trace the pattern ourselves. On the floor, using two of us as the orbiting planets walking around a central point. It was like magic. Then the second week was all about Ecology. It was led by one of the College staff members, and it included being taken for walks onto Dartmoor. She had some very interesting things to say about the entangled and vital relationship of harmony and disharmony in Nature, opposites finding brief moments of equilibrium in a constant movement."

He stops and I can feel in him both the excitement of his trip and, now, his tiredness as he pauses unable to continue with what he is saying. I think this is what Veronica was talking about at Christmas: energies, vibrations. He drinks his tea and I take the tray, leaving him to get on with his work.

"Bryony and I are planning to have lunch together, today. She's going to pick me up at about twelve."

"Sounds good," he says.

"And I might stay with her for a few days."

"That's fine. I'm not going anywhere."

I text Bryony to confirm lunch and pack my overnight bag.

It is very good to be back at the Guest House, and with Tabatha, too. After our lunch, I unpack my bag and then

Bryony and I set off for a walk along the beach. We catch up on what has happened since we were last together, and Bryony tells me that Rufus and Dotty are coming to stay.

"That's good."

"Will you stay with me when they are here?"

"If that's okay with you."

"It is."

"When will they be coming?"

"They've suggested the weekend after next."

"Good."

"Veronica said how much she had enjoyed our lunch together. How good it made her feel."

We continue our walk and come back through Thorpeness so that Bryony can buy some butter and cheese at the village shop. While we are there, we also buy two cheese and tomato tartlets for our supper. They'll go with some salad leaves.

That evening, seemingly out of nowhere, the sky darkens and the wind picks up from the south-west. By bedtime the wind is whistling through the telegraph wires. Bryony walks out onto the veranda and looks at the clouds building up behind the house. She is afraid.

"Would you mind staying here tonight?" she says. "I am becoming frightened by these storms. Somehow they seem unnatural in their fury."

"Okay. No problem."

I walk to the Guest House and gather up pyjamas, wash bag and clean underwear for the morning. I take my coat from the hook by the door and bring that with me, too.

By the time we are ready to go to bed, the storm is upon us and the house is shaking. Bryony is frightened and has pulled her duvet over her head to hide, as if not hearing the storm would make it go away. Oddly, or perhaps not oddly, I am not disturbed by the storm. Although I have to say that now that the wind has shifted to the west and is blowing against the rising tide, the height and power of the waves crashing on the shingle is humbling. Against Nature's fury, we are small and insignificant. As the waves break onto the shingle, the floorboards tremble. High tide is just after one o'clock in the morning, still three hours away, so there is much more to come. Bryony has gone to sleep, and soon I fall asleep, too. But then I am woken by a sudden crashing noise. I get up and take my torch to investigate.

The fence of the next-door house, which admittedly was somewhat broken down, has been uprooted and what is left of it is now flapping in the wind. I check my watch. It's midnight. I look out to sea. Huge white-crested waves are mounting the beach and heading towards the dune. How Bryony has not been wakened by the sounds and shaking of the storm, I cannot tell. Unlike me, she sleeps very deeply.

I put on my coat and make myself comfortable on the sofa. The house is set high above the dune so I feel safe, and I want to see the mighty force of the sea. I watch, and the tide comes to its full height, higher than I have seen it before. Then the wind drops and the ebb begins, the waves gradually slipping down the shingle bank. A strange calm replaces the storm and I fall asleep. When I wake it is six o'clock and all is quiet. I go back to bed, making sure not to wake Bryony.

I sleep through until nine o'clock to find Bryony already up and dressed. I put on my dressing gown and walk through to the kitchen, where Bryony is making toast.

"I'm afraid the wind has blown away our neighbour's fence," she says.

"Yes, I saw it."

"You saw it?"

"Yes, it woke me up just before midnight and I got up to have a look at what was happening."

"Well, I'm glad I slept through it."

Bryony makes tea while I set the table for breakfast.

"Do you think that one day the sea will take these houses?" Bryony asks. "Do you think there will come a time when the dune is overwhelmed by the sea?"

"Maybe. Perhaps one night I will be swept out of the Guest House and carried beyond the horizon."

"Can I come, too?" she says.

"Of course!" I take Bryony's hand in mine and she smiles. "Are you okay?" I ask.

"Yes, Abraham, I'm okay."

The sun is up and the sky is cloudless. Wherever the storm was, it has gone. For now, anyway.

Three days later, at around eight in the morning, Bryony and I were getting our breakfast. I walked over to the window and looked out. The sea was rough, white-topped, the wind from the north-east. The sky was overcast, grey. Then I saw it. A body. Or what looked like a body lying close to the shingle ridge. I called Bryony and she came and looked, too.

"Oh my God!"

Bryony called for an ambulance and I ran out of the house, stumbling to put on my boots and coat. It was an elderly woman, white haired, dressed in a raincoat and holding in her hand a silver photo frame. She had evidently walked into the sea. And out again. She was drenched, and shivering. I knelt beside her and covered her with my coat. She was breathing, very faintly, but she was breathing. Her face was ashen. At that moment I heard the siren of the ambulance and looking up, I saw two men clad in yellow running towards me. They were followed by a policeman and a policewoman.

I stepped back. Bryony was now standing beside me. The police woman came over to us.

"Do you know this woman?"

"Yes," said Bryony, "it's Sheila Brandon. She lives in the village, by the shop."

"And do you know who this is?" She showed us the photo that the woman had been holding.

"It's her husband," said Bryony. "He died just after Christmas."

"Do you know any of her family?"

"She has a daughter who lives in Leiston. Her name is Jessica."

"Do you know her address?"

"No, but the people in the shop will. She sometimes works part-time there."

"Thank you," said the policewoman.

"Is she okay?"

"Just about. Thank goodness you spotted her when you did."

We walked back to the house, holding each other close.

CHAPTER TWENTY-FIVE

The shock of the woman on the beach has unsettled us. We have been very quiet, not knowing what to say, or do. And now, William has texted me to say that, again, he wants me to keep an eye on his house for the next week or so. I'll stay for a night or two. Bryony says she will be okay, that in fact, she wants some time on her own. And she has Tabatha.

She drops me off at William's house, and when I arrive, William is packing his bag. I tell him about the woman on the beach.

"Thank goodness you saw her," he says.

"That's what the policewoman said. Where are you off to?"

"I'm going to stay with a friend in Norfolk who lives at Burnham Overy Staithe. It's very beautiful. The house overlooks the muddy creek-side harbour."

Apparently the creek is tidal and at high tide the water comes close to the house. His friend is a keen birdwatcher, a twitcher, and they plan to explore the marshes at Cley.

Once William has gone, I walk through the house, enjoying the stillness and the quiet of being there alone. I understand Bryony's need for time apart. I feel it, too. Is it some primal anxiety that 'feels' this need? The need to withdraw in order to recover? I don't know, but I do know it is important, necessary.

I make some tea.

CHAPTER TWENTY-SIX

When William gets back he is full of the delights of the north Norfolk coast and of how he would like to live there. This is what he does. He is very susceptible to something other than what he already has. It makes him restless. I don't think he would leave his house, but he sometimes says he will. Once, last year, it was Italy, then another time, it was Paris. If he went to Paris, it would be Suffolk, which is where he is!

I was telling William about a discussion I had had with Bryony about love, and he has given me a book by someone called Khalil Gibran. It is called *The Prophet* and apparently it is very well known, even here in Suffolk, although Khalil died a long while ago, in New York. So, here I am sitting in the garden room, reading. This is certainly something I must share with Veronica when I'm next with her. It's right up her street! I particularly like this:

When love beckons to you, follow him,
Though his ways are hard and steep.
And when his wings enfold you, yield to him,
Though the sword hidden among his pinions may wound you.

And when he speaks to you, believe him,
Though his voice may shatter your dreams as the north wind
lays waste the garden.

Although I would say, 'follow her'. I don't know why, but I think of the essential nature of Love as being feminine. I suppose it has to be both and neither.

And then he says,

But if in your fear you would seek only love's pleasure,
Then it is better for you that you cover your nakedness and
pass out of love's threshing floor.

That doesn't sound very comfortable.

CHAPTER TWENTY-SEVEN

I have been back at the Guest House for a couple of weeks. How I love this place! How I love the dawn, the sun rising above the eastern horizon and laying a path of sunlight on the water! Bryony and I had supper together last evening, and we talked about what we had found in our being together and our somewhat odd way of life. You have to understand that although we know that for you we only exist on these pages as William's fiction, to us it feels real. How else could it be? Even for someone like me, someone from another place with no past, no family and no old friends, it feels real.

Last weekend Rufus and Dotty came to stay. They drove down from London on Saturday morning and left early on Sunday evening. This time we had lunch at a new café that has opened in Thorpeness. It's called The Kitchen and serves a lot of vegetarian food, freshly prepared, locally sourced. Lots of families and dogs. It has Wi-Fi, so Clare and Rufus thought it heavenly. Then we drove to the RSPB nature reserve at Minsmere for a walk, and were lucky enough to hear a bittern booming in the reeds. I wonder if they have Wi-Fi.

Being with Rufus and Dotty is quite tiring, mostly because they are both very passionate about their work and talk about it a lot. Especially about the children who struggle with schooling designed only to measure academic achievement, whilst other bits of their lives, important bits, are ignored or dismissed.

When Rufus and Dotty left, Bryony and I went for a walk along the beach, watching the flight of the terns as they fished close to the shore-line. And then, as the water was calm, we looked for carnelian in the small stones and sand at the water's edge. As usual, I failed to see anything at all and, as usual, Bryony found two pieces, one quite small but the other the size of a pea. Once she had spotted it, she pointed to it sitting on the top of a cluster of stones shining in the evening sunlight. She picked it up, smiled at me, and put it in her pocket. I am more and more fond of Bryony. The beginnings of love? William needs to walk by the sea with Bryony.

Bryony says that my liking for comfort prevents me from becoming wise! She opens up her laptop and goes to a site called *Tricycle Magazine*, which is all about the teachings of the Buddha. Veronica suggested she looked at it. She scrolls down and there it is, an article about 'Comfort'. According to this article, comfort is a Delusion, and a liking for comfort is just the sort of thing that leads to Ignorance, which is the root cause of Suffering. It prevents us from seeing things as they are. I think that might be true, but on the other hand, I do like comfort. So, perhaps I shall have to remain a fool.

And here's another thing. Since first getting to know Bryony, and most especially since I have come to live so much of the time at the Guest House, I am beginning to feel that Bryony and I don't quite 'live together'. I think being able to do that might require something I don't have. People who really live together share the past and the future, memories and possibilities. You, dear reader, will know this, because you must be doing it all the time. But if I exist at all, I only exist in the moment. I know that since meeting Bryony I have some memories, but they are scant, and almost nothing compared to what you will have. People talk about living in the moment, but hardly anyone does. They can't. But I do. Mostly. You imagine just being here in the present. Is that what you would really want? Well, that's where I am most of the time. Just in the present.

And living by the sea changes you. It's something to do with the ever-changing patterns of wind and tide, something to do with sea-birds and the sound of the waves and the shingle. It gets inside you. And now it's inside me, and I can't 'forget' it. Do you see how I have put quotation marks around forget? That's because there is something more to the word than I can express. I hope you feel it. Forgetting means letting go, and now I can't let go of this memory. I wonder what it must be like to be like you? To have so many memories you can't count them.

CHAPTER TWENTY-EIGHT

Even though it is January and the skies are cloudy and the sea is grey, it is still good to be living by the sea. Today the wind is in the east with a touch of north. Everything I can see is horizontal, spread wide: a band of shingle, a band of sea and then sky, mostly sky. The wind is up. When the windows are shut tight, the sound of the sea is faint, muffled, but open them and the sea roars. I should keep the windows closed to keep in the warm from the radiators, but who can resist the North Sea? Not I. Bryony has gone to London to visit Veronica and I have her house to myself.

Three o'clock in the afternoon, close to high tide. The waves are running up the shingle bank, but have not reached its top, so far. The light is beginning to fade and a couple, a man and a woman, wrapped in coats and scarves are walking southwards towards Aldeburgh. She takes his arm and they walk across the shingle towards what I think must be their house just a bit further along the dune. Or, perhaps they have a car parked by the road, further down the beach. Yes, that's more likely. I haven't seen anyone else this afternoon. Too cold, the wind is too cold. It is too grey. But it is magnificent.

I have closed the windows, but all the time feel the need to open them again to let in the sea. There, I have opened one of them again. I knew I couldn't resist. In disgust, Tabatha has disappeared into Bryony's bedroom, seeking the comfort of her duvet and the blanket that covers it.

Tea. And now a lone man in a blue anorak, his hands pushed into his pockets and wearing a woolly hat walks along the shingle ridge. For less than a minute his world touches mine, although he does not know it. If the sea were to rise six feet, as some have said one day it will, it would come over the ridge and down towards the dune. But not today. I suppose when I am gone that will happen, and one day Thorpeness will be washed into the sea. Twenty past three, only about an hour of light to go. A herring gull first flies south along the water's edge, then back north.

In the dusk, a man and woman wearing matching white woolly hats walk north with a small grey dog, and the couple I thought might be walking to their car have walked back again, to the boarded pathway that leads into the village. Not residents, I think. Visitors. Three or four more gulls drifting south and then turning back against the wind. Making what they can of the last of the day's light.

The tide has turned.

I have put a shawl around my shoulders, one that Bryony uses. It carries her smell. Cloves. It is cashmere, and was made in Nepal. It is black and off-white in a herring bone pattern.

Four o'clock and the January light has almost gone, scuffs of foam left behind by the waves are carried along the beach on the wind. The man in the blue anorak passes by again, going home, head bent down against the wind. I open the window one last time to hear the sea. Ebb tide. Its roar giving way, lessening, easing into dusk. A last seagull. I am content. At one.

Four-thirty. The light has gone. Dark eventide. I am entering another realm.

I thought that the sea would quieten in the ebb, but it hasn't. Not quite a roar, but certainly a constant reminder of her cold force, her turbulence, her returning. 'I will be back,' she says. 'Come early morning, I shall be back.' I know I shall wake then, to see her return, to hear her in that bleak time between two and four; to look out of the window of the Guest House, where I shall sleep tonight. Open the window to her. Her calling. Her reminder. I am such a small thing, especially when I am on my own. I shall go to bed early and wait, sleep and wait. Tomorrow Bryony will be back.

I woke at three in the morning and opened the window of the Guest House. In the dark I could tell that the wind had dropped and the rising sea was quiet, just the incessant turning of the waves upon the shingle. She had returned, but now with her turmoil spent. I closed the window and went back to sleep, not waking till past six o'clock, by which time the tide was once more on the ebb and quieter still. I boiled the electric kettle on the table by my bed, pouring some hot water

into a cup and sat up in bed drinking the hot water. I am so
close to Mother Sea in these moments, that I feel part of her

At seven o'clock the light of day begins. Once more I open
the window, open it wide. The dark ridge of the shingle and
the faint line of the horizon are beginning to appear, but the
sun does not rise until just before eight o'clock, and anyway,
this morning it will be covered by cloud. Looking through
the open window, three quarters of the view is sky, a light
slate-grey sky with only the faintest touch of light blue. Then
a band of grey sea, and then a band of darker sandy-coloured
shingle made up of many colours.

The gulls are already up and flying to and fro along the
shore-line. The sea, now calmer, turns itself onto the beach
and draws the smaller stones back with a never-ending, pul-
sating, sigh. Out and in. Minute by minute the morning light
is returning. Now the bands of sky and sea and shingle are
clear, and I can see the pattern of waves moving towards the
water's edge. No white crests now, just the ceaseless movement of the sea in its ebb. Morning time. Another gull flies
northward, and another drifts south. A large black-backed
gull.

Seven forty-five. Daylight. One gull and then another and
then another. They fly alone, some smaller than the others.
Herring gulls and black-headed gulls, some flying low over
the waves and others turning away from the sea and flying
inland over the house. One turns and turns again, coming to
rest at the water's edge beneath the shingle bank, and then
takes off again. More and more of them. Out at sea, a flock of
four black birds flies northwards in loose formation. I cannot

say what they are. Just four birds flying low over the water. Probably geese.

I get out of bed. I am still in my dressing gown, but now I put on a cardigan and then a pair of socks, my overcoat and woolly hat and shoes, and taking my stick I walk over the shingle bank and down to the water's edge. The tide has fallen to show a strip of hard sand, and now, to my right, I can see a cluster of gulls fishing in the shallow water. It is cold, but without the bitterness of the north and east wind. No one else is up, although there is light in the upper floor of one of the houses set back away from the dune. I feel at home.

Breakfast. And then Bryony will come home, back to her house by the sea.

PART FOUR

ABRAHAM
AND BRYONY

CHAPTER TWENTY-NINE

Veronica called this morning to ask her mother if she and I would like to take a trip to Paris. The Harmonia Quartet is going to be playing in a concert, and that she would like us to be there. Of course, we both want to go. However, I am not quite sure how this works, and I think I shall have to speak to William.

When I arrive at William's house, he is in his study and, having said hello, I ask him if he has a moment to talk to me.

"Yes, of course." He stands up. "Would you like some tea?"

"Yes, thank you."

We walk into the kitchen and William puts the kettle on the hob while I get the large brown teapot from the shelf and then two of the white mugs from the cupboard. Both William and I drink our tea black. We take our mugs and sit down.

"Now, Abraham, what can I do for you?"

"Well, Bryony and I want to go to Paris."

"Paris?"

"Yes, Veronica is playing in a concert in Paris and she would like us to be there. Bryony thought we might go by train. I think it's called the Eurostar."

"Yes, it is. I use it quite often."

"Do you? I don't remember you ever telling me about it."

"Well, I don't tell you everything I do."

"No, I guess you don't. Anyway, Bryony and I think it likely that we can't go to Paris without you writing it down. So, we want to know whether you will do that."

William smiles. "It is odd, isn't it? You are quite certain you want to go, but you cannot actually do it on your own. That is strange."

"I suppose it is. I'm so used to it, I don't think about it."

"Well, sometimes you seem to have lives of your own, and then sometimes not."

He stands up and takes his mug back into the kitchen.

"But you know," he says, "I have felt recently that your lives are becoming increasingly intertwined and that I am not entirely able to shape them. It's as if you are growing away from me. A bit. I don't mind, but that's how it feels."

"Do you think so? I do feel very comfortable with Bryony. What about Paris, then?"

"Yes, Paris is fine. I guess Bryony will organise the tickets and find a hotel. She can do it online."

"Probably."

"Okay. Let me know how it goes."

"Won't you know?"

"Well, I'm not sure. Tell me anyway."

"Okay."

146

Bryony has bought the tickets. We have to catch an early train to get to London on time for the Eurostar train from St Pancras International. William is going to take us to the station in Saxmundham. The journey to Paris from London takes just over two and a half hours, and the train departs at 12.25, meaning we will have time to go to our hotel and change before going to the concert. Veronica wants us to have supper with her afterwards to meet the rest of the quartet and some of their Parisian friends. It all sounds very exciting.

We are on our way and Bryony and I have a great sense of adventure.

"You see what happens?" I say to Bryony. "I live this dull life. Then I meet you and have chocolate in Orford and now a concert and supper in Paris."

"To say nothing of violent storms and a body on the beach in Thorpeness!"

"No, indeed. By the way, what happened to that poor woman?"

"Sheila Brandon? They took her to Ipswich hospital. No bones broken, but quite severe hypothermia. Thank goodness we saw her when we did. I spoke to her daughter in the village shop the other day and she said that her mother had recovered – at least from the hypothermia. She continues to grieve. When we get back, I'll go and visit her. We can compare notes."

We have arrived at St Pancras in good time and have found our seats. There are a great many people on the train and a lot of luggage, and I am beginning to realise that I am not at all used to this kind of adventure. I'm being taken out of my comfort zone by the agitation of the crowds, and I seem to be jumping at every sudden noise. Fortunately, Bryony seems to be very much at ease, as if this is the sort of thing she does all the time. And probably, she once did.

Anyway, the train sets off and soon we are travelling at what seems to be a great speed. About four times as fast as the little train that runs from Saxmundham to Ipswich! We pass through Kent almost in a blur and then plunge into the tunnel under the Channel. Twenty minutes later we are in France. Just twenty minutes! For some reason I am very excited about being in France and immediately look for cars driving on the right. It's as if I have a boyish memory, which I assume I don't have, of being 'abroad' for the first time.

Soon we are pulling into the Gare du Nord station and after waiting in a long queue, which twists and turns back on itself and then forward again, we take a taxi to our hotel. We are driven through more noise, madness and mayhem. I have never seen so many cars, buses and scooters criss-crossing in front of each other, their horns blaring. I keep thinking we will all end up entangled in each other's bumpers, but we don't, and in a chaotic way we pass between, in front and behind each other until we reach our hotel. We register and are taken to a large double room with a bathroom. It's on the second floor of the hotel and we overlook a tree-lined boulevard. There is a café opposite with a red awning over tables set on a wide pavement, where people are still enjoying their lunch. Bryony says it's very French, and she would know because she has danced in Paris.

We unpack, wash and change into our concert-going clothes. I have to tell you that Bryony looks very lovely in a deep blue dress and a silver-white shawl, her hair drawn up and held in a silver clasp. High heels. She has painted her nails pink. I like that. I, too, am in dark blue. I look a bit less loose and baggy than normal. I have not painted my nails, but I am wearing on my jacket my bumblebee pin from the Bumblebee Conservation Trust of which I am fond – the pin that is, not the Trust. We have both taken an overcoat in case it is colder after the concert and I have to say we look quite smart. Almost Parisian. Although how should I know what being 'Parisian' is?

We are now at the concert hall surrounded by chatter as people find their seats and wave to friends. We are about four rows back from the stage and I have an aisle seat, which I like. I can always escape.

The lights dim and Harmonia walk on stage. This evening they are dressed in deep red evening gowns, with thin shoulder straps, and with shiny black and silver beads woven into their hair. The programme is to be shorter than the one in Snape and with no interval. Fortunately, I went to the loo before we took our seats. There are to be three pieces: Mozart's String Quartet in G Major, a short piece by Mendelssohn, and then Haydn. This time the Haydn is Opus 42 in D Minor. I do not cry, but am full of delight. Delight in the music, delight in the sight of these four talented young women, and delight in being here with Bryony in a concert hall in Paris. From time to time, we turn and smile at each other, and then Bryony reaches out and takes my hand in hers. This is very good. I am content. Do you remember what I said about 'happiness'? Well, this isn't happiness, this is much closer to a deep sense of being at one.

The concert has ended and now we are having supper. Veronica has booked a table in a restaurant that is only a short walk from the concert hall. Arm in arm we are taken there. There is our table, candlelit. And now we are ordering wine and food. Well, Veronica is ordering the wine and we are looking at the menu. There is not much of a choice for vegetarians, but when I tell the patron that I prefer vegetarian food, he simply says: "Leave this to me."

I did not know there was food like this! I have been presented with a dish of roasted vegetables and halloumi cheese set on a cushion of the most wonderful mashed potato, and with a mysterious but delicious sauce. It is almost beyond food. I find that I am smiling, out of control smiling.

The conversation is all about music and concerts and living in Paris. Veronica's friends are trying to persuade her to come and live in France. They are young and full of life and passion. There is a wondrous graceful movement about them. I sit and listen and watch. I am so glad we came to Paris, and for a moment I feel sure I could live here, although probably couldn't. I would miss the quiet of Aldeburgh and the ebb and flow of the tide. Yes, I would. But I will remember this evening. You see William, how this goes? Another memory.

At about eleven-thirty Bryony says we must go to bed, and we stand up to leave. I am kissed on the cheek by all of the beautiful young women, which is a treat, and I get a special hug from Veronica. We take a taxi back to our hotel, and we go to our room. We go to bed. We sleep. Our train tomorrow is not until lunchtime, so we won't have to rush our breakfast. Veronica will be there for a couple more days.

We set off on the Eurostar and are soon back in London. We take a taxi to Liverpool Street and catch an evening train to Saxmundham, where we have arranged to be met by the Squirrel Taxi. Now, tired by our journey, we are sitting in Bryony's house. Bryony has been very quiet today. I haven't said anything, but I want to let her know I have noticed.

"What a journey," I say. "Are you okay?"

"Yes, I'm okay, Abraham, but sometimes when I see Veronica flourishing and happy, I think about how much her father would have liked to see her."

"Yes, of course."

"And then I find myself in a place of memory and sadness. And sometimes it feels just unfair. Why us? Why did this happen to us? Why did Veronica have to lose a father she loved so much?" She stands and goes into the kitchen. "Anyway, I'm tired now and must sleep."

"I'll go to the Guest House."

"Okay. I'll see you in the morning. I am so glad you came with me to Paris. And I'm glad you're here now."

"Me too."

CHAPTER THIRTY

The next weekend Veronica was coming to stay with her mother, and thinking they would like some time on their own, I went back to William's house on the Thursday evening. I wanted to catch up with him, tell him about Paris. No sooner was I there than I got a text from Bryony inviting me to tea on Saturday. So, I was back at Sandy Bar by three-thirty that afternoon. After tea, Veronica and I went for a walk along the beach, Veronica taking my arm in that way that she does. We walked for a bit, not talking, but then Veronica asked me a question that took me by surprise.

"Abraham, do you know what it feels like to be loved?"

For a moment, I couldn't answer, but then I did.

"Being who I am, Veronica, this is not such an easy question to answer."

"Have you ever loved someone?"

"Well, not really. The closest I've come to what I think love might be is with your mother."

"Do you love each other?"

"Well, we are very fond of each other and we enjoy being together. I find our times together very special. And perhaps that's because we also have time apart."

We walked on.

"Why are you asking me about love?"

A long pause.

"I suppose it's about Alex and me."

"Do you love each other?"

"Yes, I think we do, but there are times when it…I don't know… times when it disappears."

"Disappears?"

"Yes. You see, as I think you know by now, I often inhabit a deep inner realm of being. It's what helps me play the violin. When I'm playing, I draw from within myself a great depth of feeling and intensity, and sometimes it is almost as if I have entered another place. It's astonishing."

"And Alex?"

"He doesn't have it. He plays well. He has good technique and he can feel the needs of the music, what it is trying to say, but he doesn't have that inner depth. He just can't find it."

"And how does this affect your love for each other?"

"That is what I ask myself."

Veronica stops to pick up a grey, round pebble, with a white mark on it, which she holds in her hand and then throws into the sea. Plop! She looks at me as if she is hoping I might have something to say to her, but I don't.

"Sometimes when we are together," she says, "especially if I am tired or preoccupied, I withdraw into myself. And when I do that, I think Alex feels abandoned. Then nothing he says brings us together. The opposite. It seems to increase the distance between us."

We stop again and then turn back towards the house.

"Have you asked Alex about this, asked him what he is feeling when it happens?"

"Not really. It passes. Sometimes it might last for a day

or two, but then it passes and we are as we were before, close, loving, working together at our music."

"Perhaps that is how it has to be?"

"Perhaps."

When we get to the house, Veronica's mobile has been ringing. It's Alex. He has left a message to say how much he is missing her, hoping that she is enjoying her weekend and sending his love.

A day or two later, Bryony and I are having lunch together at The Kitchen. Just soup and bread, but homemade vegetable soup and fresh sourdough bread.

"Did you enjoy having Veronica to stay?"

"Yes, it was good. And she shared with me the conversation she had with you on your walk along the beach."

"I hope she felt loved by Alex's message on her mobile."

"She did, but I think that this shift in mood is something she will have to learn to live with. I did. Odd really, first the mother and then the daughter. But for me it was the other way around."

"What do you mean?"

"Her father was like that. Sudden shifts in mood. Sometimes he seemed overtaken by a darkness, and it could happen out of nowhere. We would be fine in the morning. I would go out to do some shopping and when I came back I could hardly talk to him. It was as if he was somewhere else. It never lasted long, but while it lasted the darkness was impenetrable."

"What did you do?"

"I put up with it, and I learnt not to try and bring him back. He came back in his own time and said nothing about it."

"I sometimes feel a bit down," I say.

"Yes, of course, but that is not the same thing."

"Isn't it?"

"No, not the same thing at all."

She calls for the bill. I want to talk more about this, but I sense that she does not. The conversation is over. For the time being anyway.

"Could you drop me off at William's house?"

"Yes, of course."

We arrive, and then as I am getting out of the car Bryony asks me if I intend to return to the Guest House.

She says, "I think Tabatha might be missing you."

I say, "I want to spend a bit more time with William, but I'd like to come back in a couple of days if that's okay?"

"That would be lovely. Shall we go to Orford?"

"Alright. Why don't you pick me up on Friday morning and we'll go from there. I'll pack a bag so that I can stay for a while."

"Sounds good."

Left on my own, I find myself thinking about what Bryony has said about her husband's darkness. She is so open that it must have been difficult for her to feel his closure. And no doubt, by being there for him she gave him strength, knowing that she would be there when the darkness passed. Don't you think? But then what about her need to be loved and cherished? But she speaks of him so fondly that I think he must have given her that, too. In his own way. I hope so.

CHAPTER THIRTY-ONE

Bryony and I are now spending most of our time together in her house by the sea. And I like sleeping in the Guest House, especially for the solitude of the morning time. In recent weeks, my sleeping patterns seem to have become very particular, so that I now look forward to being awake in the early morning, between two o'clock and six o'clock, and then getting up just before seven. To balance this, I am going to bed shortly after nine o'clock in the evening and take a nap after lunch for about an hour. Bryony and I have also made it a habit to eat only at breakfast and lunch time with a glass of red wine and then a small snack at about six in the evening. I eat small amounts. And all in all, I feel somehow lighter. We are making our own patterns.

Each day, we walk along the beach, either north towards Dunwich or south towards Aldeburgh. Our days have become uncluttered, easy to live, and somehow or other we are content. Today, we are going to have lunch at the Snape Maltings and then we shall walk through the marshes towards Iken.

I know that we are both a fiction, characters brought to the page by William, but as our life together takes shape it is as if we are creating a world of our own. Something almost untouched by him. It is as if our lives lie as much in our imagination as in his. I suppose that cannot be, but that is what it feels like. Where I come from, these matters seldom arise. I think I will have to tell Bryony about it.

Driving back to Thorpeness, I turn to Bryony, sitting upright at the wheel as she always does.

"Did you enjoy your lunch?"

"Yes, I did, although it was a bit noisy."

"That's true. Do you think we are making a world of our own?"

"Well, if we are it is one in which we prefer to be quiet."

We laugh – quietly. No, we laugh out loud. Laughter is part of being with Bryony.

"I notice," I say, "that when we are in your house by the sea, there is always the sound of the waves on the shingle, and that because of this, everything else goes quiet. It's as if the sound of the sea is enough. Nothing else needs to be said."

"Almost nothing!"

"Yes, almost nothing."

"You and I talk a lot don't we?" she says. "I know we can be together for a long time and say nothing, but we do talk a lot. You know, about how we are feeling, whether we are okay, what we have just done and what we might do next."

"Hardly earth-shattering is it?"

"No not earth-shattering. There's quite enough of that going on elsewhere!"

Again we laugh. Louder this time. Do you see what is happening, William?

When we get to the house, we sit on the veranda. I decide this is the moment.

"Bryony," I say, "there is something I must tell you. Something about me."

She looks at me wondering what I am going to say.

"You're not unwell are you?"

"No, nothing like that. It's about where I come from."

She waits for me to continue.

"You see, in a way we are both characters written down by William. He has brought us to the page and he shapes our lives, but as I think you know, there are times when we live our lives for ourselves – we tell the story."

"Yes, that's right. I have felt that part of our lives growing around us."

"But there's something else. You see, there is a difference between us. I am something other than this. I come from another place – the world of spirit. I am part of who William has always been and always will be; part of who he will become. In fact, that's my task, to lead him to the place he seeks."

"And where is that?"

"It's here, Bryony. The place he seeks is here. It is you."

"I don't understand…"

"Well, what William seeks is Love. He wants to love and be loved. And for him, this is what you represent. Love. That is why he has created you, and I am trying to show him the way. He has a long way to go, but that is why I am here."

Bryony stands up and moves towards the archway of the veranda, leaning against it. Then she lets out a long sigh and sits on the steps.

"So, is this all make-believe? You and me. Does it mean nothing to you?"

"Oh no, it's not make-believe at all. It is more real than anything else. It wouldn't work if it were otherwise. I am falling in love with you. That is how it has to be. But it is how it is anyway. This part of William that is me, is falling in love with you."

159

"And am I falling in love with you or with William?"

"For now, it is me. But there may come a time where there will be no difference. William and Abraham; Abraham and William. Only you and I will know the difference."

For a while we say nothing more. But then Bryony stands up and comes and sits beside me again. She takes my hand.

"I suppose that I am not free to choose?"

"I'm not sure," I say. "I'm not sure. None of this has been written down as yet."

Bryony stands and goes to walk back into the house.

"Well, we will see. We will see."

CHAPTER THIRTY-TWO

It occurs to me that William has done something very odd in making me as I am, a man without family and without a past. An isolated person dropped on to the page, coming, as he supposes, from nowhere. He has set me alone and, at the same time, seeks to make me dependent on him. But William is not God, whoever that is, and he cannot create a separate world, my world. And if I am a fiction, then the world he has ordained for me must be a fiction, too. But is that all it is? After all, dear reader, I don't know you and never will, but you are real. Presumably. And where is the 'real' world anyway? I have no idea, but I suspect it lies in 'the gaps between'; the gaps between those things we take to be real. This chair, that bowl, your cushion, Bryony's hand on mine. The truth is – here comes the truth – there is no separate 'real world'. Not for me, not for William, and not for you, because everything exists in some kind of continuous cosmic community. I don't know how I know this, but I do know it's true. I see it in the sunrise and I hear it in the sighing of the waves upon the shingle. I feel it in the love that is now arising between Bryony and me and in the withdrawn darkness of Veronica. Which of those moments is true and which only an illusion?

I don't know why I am like this today. Bryony has gone to London to stay with Veronica for a couple of days, so I am sitting here on her veranda talking to myself. And to you dear reader. Take no notice. Sometimes these thoughts come to me and then they are there, until they cease to be – no more real or unreal than any other thought. I think they are going to a show in the West End, a musical. Bryony will tell me all about it when she returns. I have decided to stay at the Guest House, and I woke this morning to a clear sky, the sun rising above the horizon and laying its path on the water, commanded by the Cosmos.

I woke, as I often do, alone and with a feeling of unease. My dreams have disturbed me, although I cannot remember them. Does that ever happen to you? Seven o'clock. It is very still. I feel a bit sick. I've noticed that, just recently. When I wake up, I feel a bit sick. Perhaps I should see the doctor – or just imagine that I am well. One or the other. Anyway, I met someone the other day. He is a friend of William's and he had been visiting his brother in Southwold, just up the coast. His name is Joseph, and I liked him. I had been staying for a couple of days with William and Joseph called in to see him. William introduced me to Joseph over a cup of tea. He is a philosopher and a theologian. He and William talked about his work and the book Joseph is writing on Natural Law. Something to do with Thomas Aquinas. It seems that Joseph has a deep knowledge and understanding of Plato and of Aristotle, hence his book, I suppose. He knows about that time before the Enlightenment. Apparently, his ideas are not at all fashionable in 'our profane, mechanistic and materialist world, with its quest for measurement and certainty, with its dominant economic literalism'. William's words, not mine. How should I know such a thing?

Anyway, I was drawn to Joseph at once. He is a small man, bearded with long hair and mischievous eyes. He was very funny talking about these things, mocking himself for his contrary views, or rather mocking the ways things are thought to be, the absurdities of what we now claim to be true, our blind separation, our stridency, our arrogance. But his mocking was kind, even compassionate. He had brought with him a couple of his essays on Justice and Harmony, and I asked William to make copies of them for me. I have them here. I wish you could read them. They tell of a world we have forgotten and which yet, in the telling, is familiar. I have never read anything like this before – not that that says much. But oddly, as I read it I felt I knew what I was reading, and I wonder whether you would, too. According to Joseph, there was a time, a Golden Age, when we experienced without question our relationship with Nature and with the Cosmos. We didn't think it, we just knew it. That sounds familiar somehow. But now we can't do that. We have to work it out for ourselves in our heads. And yet there are moments here on the shingle and by the sea when I feel it. Just feel it. Does that happen to you?

Everything is a fiction. There is nothing other than what we make up for ourselves. We make things as they are. As the Buddha once said, 'With our thoughts we make the world.' William told me that, too. We make the world with our thoughts and then that is all there is. My made-up world, dear reader, bumps up against yours. And when they meet we touch. For a moment or two we touch. Then we part.

Now I am wondering when Bryony will come home. I miss her.

CHAPTER THIRTY-THREE

Bryony is back and she has brought Veronica with her. They arrived late yesterday evening, driving themselves from the station where Bryony had parked her car. They'd had a lovely time. They saw the musical 'An American in Paris' at the Dominion Theatre. Lots of dancing and well-known songs. In the interval they had each drunk a large gin and tonic, and then giggled. They are very easy with each other. That must be a wonderful thing. Mother and daughter just enjoying being togther. Although Veronica does not dance, her love of music brings her close to her mother and they talk about performances and audiences. Veronica has just come back from giving her Masterclass to students in the Faculty of Music at the University of Oxford. Apparently, she has been doing this each year for the last two years. More vibrations, different energies. Then she comes home and gets on with the rest of her life.

Worlds bumping into each other and then parting. Being with and then parting. Moving from one place to another. Living with Bryony, living by the sea, talking to Veronica, I am learning. Not so much for myself, for where I come from this is already known, but for William. Do you see? I am helping William learn how to be with someone and what it means to be in 'place'. To stay in one place and enjoy being there. Being and learning.

Sometimes I cannot separate myself at all. Sometimes when I sit in bed with Bryony in the stillness and silence of the morning, when we read or just talk to each other about the day to come, I slip and lose any sense of myself, the alone self. And then, at other times, when I am in the Guest House, I know I am apart. On my own. But always the sea, the beach and the sea. The shingle bank and the water's edge, waves, seagulls squawking. If you sit quietly, on your own, it doesn't matter where, if you sit quietly, nothing but heartbeat and breathing… close your eyes…Where are you? For me, by the sea.

Bryony has made tea and toast and is sitting at her table. Veronica is asleep in her attic bedroom. I can tell that Bryony wants to tell me about the show and I want to tell her about my meeting with Joseph. We will, but just for now there is nothing to be said. Just settling back in. Coming together again.

It is mid-morning and Veronica has appeared in her dressing gown. Bryony is making her tea, and I ask her about her Masterclass. She turns her head and looks out towards the sea, cupping her chin in her hands, elbows on the table. She catches my gaze and smiles at me.

"The odd thing is that the young people who came – about fifteen in all – were very serious-minded. I had somehow supposed that they would be light-hearted and passionate, but they were not. Not at all. Dedicated, yes, but rather humour-less and even dull. Is that what this generation has become?"

"Perhaps," says Bryony, who has now brought Veronica her tea and is standing beside her. "They have to work so hard to get to university, and they'll probably finish up without a job and in debt. Not much to be light-hearted about, I suppose."

"Well, anyway, two or three of them were super good. One young man, in particular. I would think he'd have no difficulty getting into one of the European symphony orchestras, or even American. Of all of them, he was by far and away the most energetic. Which is good. Actually, it's essential."

Bryony lays her hand gently on Veronica's shoulder and Veronica reaches up and takes her hand.

"Did they call you 'Maestro'?"

"No they did not! They called me Veronica."

"Which, of course, is who you are."

We laugh, both Bryony and I enjoying the evident love between them.

"Does anyone fancy a walk?" I ask.

'I'd love that," says Veronica.

Then Bryony says, "Why don't you take Abraham for a walk, darling, and I'll stay here?"

"Okay. Is he in need of exercise?"

"I am," I say.

I take my coat from the hook by the door and Veronica runs upstairs, coming back wrapped in a long overcoat, a scarf and a red woolly hat.

"I don't think it is quite that cold," I say.

"It is if you live in London and are unfamiliar with the east wind."

She takes my arm and we set off, walking over the shingle bank, northwards along the sea-shore. For a while we say nothing, but then Veronica looks at me and smiles.

167

"You know, although I did find the young musicians somewhat dull, I also admire them. As I said, they are dedicated to their work, but there's something else. They seem to be much more comfortable with themselves than I remember being at that age. They seem to be content with who they are."

"What do you mean?"

"Well, I hope you won't mind me saying this..."

"I'll try not to."

"It's just that when I was their age, I was much more taken up with my sexuality than they seem to be. Sex was a big thing and there was a lot of it going on. This generation seems to take their sexuality for granted, they make nothing of it, and one of the young women was telling me that it doesn't matter much to her. It wasn't that she didn't have sexual friendships, but that's what they were, friendships. And I don't mean casual friendships; she told me they were committed to each other, but the sex bit was not really what their friendships were about. She was talking very openly about gender, or rather, telling me that they are just not preoccupied with it."

That's interesting. Do you remember that I discussed something like this with William? Well, I do, but I don't say anything about it to Veronica. Somehow it doesn't seem quite right for someone as old as me to have an opinion on how these young people live their lives. We continue with our walk, Veronica taking my arm as if I might have been her father, which I should have liked to have been.

After about half an hour, we turn and begin to walk back. I ask Veronica about her plans for the coming months, and she tells me she is thinking about going to Paris. There is the possibility that the BBC might be partnering an exchange with the Orchestre de Paris, but it's very early days and in the meantime she has concerts in London and the quartet are going to take part in a festival in Berlin. Her life sounds so exciting to me. Apart from my trip to Paris with Bryony, William has kept me here on the Suffolk coast. Of course, I love it, but I feel her excitement.

When we reach the house, we can see Bryony moving in and out of the kitchen.

"She looks content," I say.

"She does, and I believe she is."

We have lunch and then each of us goes our own way. I am reading on the veranda, Bryony is on her laptop and Veronica is doing something in her attic room. The afternoon passes and then it is supper time. Bryony and I prepare and lay the table. We have a vegetable quiche and salad. Wine. Laughter. And then we talk. At about nine-thirty, Veronica takes herself off to bed, and Bryony and I sit for a while together.

"How was Veronica on your walk?" Bryony asks me.

"She was fine. Rather relaxed, I thought. She was talking about gender."

"What about it?"

"Well, it seems that young people are now much less prepared to be shaped by the stereotypes of gender. They like to relate to each other for who they are, not as their gender dictates."

We sit for a while looking out into the dark of the night.

"I once made a joke about all of that to William."

"A joke about gender?"

"Well, sort of. I'd been reading some stuff on his computer about these changing attitudes, and I said I had decided to have no gender at all. I meant it as a joke, but having listened to Veronica, it's made me think again."

"In what way?"

"Well, I wasn't thinking about how young people see gender. After all, I have no way of knowing about that. I was thinking about the loss of gender – not about a man deciding to become a woman, or a woman wanting to be a man, but a man or a woman wanting neither. Not wanting to be defined by either. Do you think that if young people grow up rejecting the old stereotypes of what it is to be a man or a woman they might shed their gender altogether? Not their sexuality, I'm not suggesting that, but their gender. Might that lead to a more harmonious and peaceable world, do you think?"

"I find that difficult to imagine."

"Yes it is, isn't it, and perhaps that's the point. But then I thought of something else."

"Wow, you have been busy."

"I thought about what happens when we get older."

"You mean like you and me?"

"Yes, like you and me. Or at least the you and me that William has made. That *is* something I know about."

"And?"

"And, what I notice is that as we get older we become more and more like each other. We remain who we are, woman and man, but we become more like each other. You know, some of what it is to be a man leaves men and some of what it is to be a woman leaves women. This has nothing to do with beauty or how, for example, I feel attracted to you. Those feelings remain. But it's about the way we are, how we become closer. I think as we age gender begins to slip away."

Bryony looks across towards me and smiles.

"And on that note," she says, "I think we should go to bed. I wonder who I shall wake up with in the morning? Will it be you? And which you will it be?"

We laugh and go to bed, taking each other in our arms, enfolded, laughing. Tenderness.

The next morning, Veronica returns to London.

CHAPTER THIRTY-FOUR

I have noticed something – something that is happening to me. At first, when William placed me upon the page, I felt as if I was little more than a mouthpiece for his thoughts. Do you remember that? I remember looking at papers in his study, looking at what he had been working on, taking an interest in *his* life and what *he* was doing. Dependent upon him. But as I have been telling you, recently that has begun to go away, and as I have come to live with Bryony for so much of my time (not *my time* as I have said before, just mornings and afternoons and nights, moments in a day – well, I suppose that is my time), and as I have begun to have memories of my own, I have come to see myself not so much simply as a fiction created by William, but *as someone who lives with Bryony*. Have you noticed that?

My life and my sense of who I am is now shaped by our being together, and I note that I have begun to ponder on my own thoughts, to ponder by myself and for myself. Reflection. Isn't that what makes us unique? Well, I have come to reflect and ponder. Not all the time, but it is making that part of me that is shaped by William smaller and that part of me which is free is spreading its wings. I know I am leading William to

Bryony, my appointed task, but even as I do so, something else is arising in me – and in Bryony, too. And it's not about William.

Then this morning, when I woke in the Guest House and pulled up the blind to see the North Sea, I remembered something. I was a boy, perhaps ten or eleven years old, and I was lying under an apple tree in a sloping orchard. It must have been early summer. The apple blossom was full and pink and white, the grass was long. In that moment, looking up into the branches or down at me, the apple tree and I became one. We were in some strange way absorbed into one another. I can't make out whether that was a dream or a memory.

CHAPTER THIRTY-FIVE

When the wind is down and the tide is low, lying beneath the shingle bank, the sea is quiet. It makes only a very gentle sound as the waves, one after the other, turn onto the shore. Then as the wind rises, so does the sound of the sea's turning. Two sounds: the first is fainter, more distant and continuous and seems to come from further up the shoreline; the second is nearby, deeper and regular with pauses in between as the waves 'thrump' upon the sand, a low, dull, heavy sound, one wave in seven being larger and noisier than the others. Always the sea, moving. And from morning till night-time gulls fly, turn and swoop over the waves.

This morning, sitting on the veranda waiting for Bryony to shower and dress, I am facing towards the sun and I feel its warmth. I am wearing my coat because the south-easterly wind is cold, but nevertheless, the warmth of the sun is on my face, and its light is spread in a wide path upon the water, reviving my spirit, my sense of being part of something, some kind of cosmic consciousness that makes me part of The Whole. In this moment, in this single and particular moment, I am at peace.

CHAPTER THIRTY-SIX

I cannot quite believe what has been happening this summer. Bryony and I have been together all the time. Not doing much, just passing the time.

We have added something else to our routine. On Sunday mornings we read in bed. The routine is that I sleep with Bryony on a Saturday night and then at eight on the Sunday morning, I get up, put on my dressing gown, and make two mugs of tea. We put the mugs on our bedside tables and then we sit in bed, propped up by our pillows, and read. I read detective stories, and Bryony reads fiction, mostly written by young British authors, many of them women. Books that have been recommended to her by Johnny and Mary in the Aldeburgh Bookshop. She has become very interested in what is being written by these young authors, often their first novel. And sometimes, if there is a book she particularly likes, she passes it on to me, so that I, too, can discover what they are writing about, how they see the world. This world. Now. Perhaps because I have no past, I am not interested in books about what might have happened before now.

Anyway, that is what we do on Sunday mornings. Sometimes I fall back to sleep, which is especially delicious. And then we get up, shower and dress, and at about eleven-thirty, go for a walk. We have discovered another delight, Mel's Café in Aldeburgh. It's tucked away by the garden centre off the Saxmundham road, and is mainly used by local people, not visitors. The food is very good, home-cooked. The café is heaven, small and warm and steamy. It smells of cooking and comfort. There is only one room, the kitchen, and the blue serving counter, with its plates of shortbread and almond tarts, opening up to eight tables set close together, three round, the others square, chairs pushed in. Behind the counter is Mel, wearing her apron and cooking at a slow pace, and Caroline taking orders and making teas and coffees. Sometimes we have vegetable soup with thick sourdough toast. The bread comes from a man in Theberton whose bakery is a shed in his garden. This is food to make you smile. And we do. Then we have Mel's apple crumble and custard. Ecstasy!

After lunch we come back to the house. I sleep and Bryony does whatever it is that she wants to do, looking at stuff on her laptop, and sometimes ironing. She loves ironing. I have other tasks, such as hoovering, which I like and which includes plumping the cushions, which I also like, filling and emptying the dishwasher and making sure there is salt in the water softener. But Bryony has a love of laundry and ironing. She says it is like a meditation. Imagine that! I am not allowed to speak to her when she is ironing. She enters a different realm. In the evening, we watch Netflix. Have you tried it? There's an endless list of things to watch, either films or TV series, or documentaries. All sorts. I, of course, like crime and mystery, not violent but something with good characters and a plot. Bryony likes documentaries, travel and natural history. We don't much mind. It's the doing it together that we like, and then talking about it. And I think we do it just for us.

We like Sundays.

CHAPTER THIRTY-SEVEN

Bryony and I are walking along the beach. After breakfast, we walked all the way to Aldeburgh and went to the bookshop, and now we are walking home carrying our books, eager to begin reading. I have suggested that we leave the path and walk along the water's edge, closer to the sea and now we have stopped for a while and are sitting on the shingle ridge looking out towards the horizon. Just looking. Seagulls flying.

I've been thinking. I have things I want to say. I put my arm through Bryony's and we come close.

"I guess there's a risk in all of this," I say.

She turns and looks at me. "What are you talking about?"

"Us, I'm talking about us. There's a risk. I see it now."

"What kind of risk?"

"Well, before – before us – I never gave it a thought. I just went from one thing to another. There was no connection between one day and another, just this day and then this one. Apart from William and Tabatha, I was not attached to anyone. Never had been. I had no memory of anything, only of what had happened yesterday, and no thought about the future, either. Just today. But now that has changed."

"And?"

"And there's a risk."

I stood up and walked down to the water's edge.

"Let's get home," says Bryony.

"Okay."

We walk back in silence, Bryony holding my arm. Then up and over the shingle and to the house. When we reach the veranda, I sit down on one of the rattan chairs, turning my face to the late morning sun, and Bryony comes and sits beside me, putting our books on the table. She takes my hand.

"You know, Abraham, when I hear you talk like that, about the risk of being in love, I wonder whether it's you speaking, or William."

"What do you mean?"

"Well, we are both creations of William's imagination and to that extent we express not what we feel, but what he feels. And we both know he has a problem with loving and being loved. The 'risk' of it all is just the sort of thing that he would feel, not you."

"Yes, that's right. It is exactly how he would feel."

"And yet, somehow or other, in being together we have grown beyond him. We have, haven't we?"

"Yes, we have."

"So now, where is the risk? In us or in William?"

I am often astonished at the way in which Bryony sees into things, sees them as they are. Sometimes she astounds me with her insight, and somehow the part of me which is Abraham feels unworthy of it. Silly, I know, but it's true. How is it that I have found my way here?

Bryony stands up and unlocks the door to the house. She goes in and I remain, feeling the warmth of the sun. After a while, Bryony comes back carrying a tray with two mugs of soup and some oatcakes. Lunch.

"You know, my darling Abraham," she says, "it's the most natural thing in the world."

"What is?"

"Loving and being loved."

"It is?"

"Yes, it is. It's what we are meant to do. Love one another. It's just that William doesn't trust it, so he projects his mistrust onto you. But you and I know that being in love is just that; being *in* love. And when you dwell *in* it, it is always there."

"That's completely wonderful, Bryony. Wonderful. How have you learnt that?"

"I didn't, it was given to me."

"By whom?"

"Many people. And, as it happens, one of them is you."

"Really?"

"Yes, really."

We laugh and I nearly spill my soup.

"Do you think it gets any better than this?" I ask.

"I doubt it," she says.

That night, Bryony and I sleep together and when we wake, early, the sun is once more, miraculously, lifting off the horizon. We make porridge and we carry our bowls on to the veranda, where we sit eating it. Neither of us needs to say anything; we are in a state of complete ease, deep peacefulness. And porridge. If comfort is not for the wise, we must have become very foolish. We are at one.

CHAPTER THIRTY-EIGHT

I have been staying with Bryony for almost three months now, only going back to William's house from time to time to change clothes or just catch up with him. But today he has sent me a text message to say he wants me back at his house. Bryony takes me in her car.

When I walk into the house it is very quiet, but then I can hear William talking to someone on the phone. I sit in the living room and notice my tapestry leaning against the arm of one of the chairs. William must have seen me coming up the garden path because as soon as he finishes his telephone call he walks through.

"Ah, Abraham, there you are."

"Yes, here I am. At your command, I think."

"Yes, at my command, although I have begun to wonder if that is still true."

I feel as if I am being told off, but I just sit there and say nothing, waiting to discover what it is that William wants to tell me. He seems upset by something and he goes into the kitchen and pours himself a glass of water from the jug in the fridge. Filtered water. He comes back and sits opposite me in the armchair against which my tapestry is leaning. I don't know why I think that detail is important, but somehow it is.

"Abraham," he says, "when I first put you onto the page, and when I then introduced you to Bryony, I didn't suppose that she would take you from me."

What?!!

"Of course, I wanted you to have a friend, have some company other than me, but I had supposed that you would still live here for most of the time. Maybe I should have seen it coming: chocolate in Orford, the phone, and that trip to Paris…But I hadn't thought you would be living with her. It's almost as if you have fallen in love."

"I have fallen in love. We have, Bryony and I. It's not that difficult if you let it happen."

William looks away. I have touched a spot. That, of course, is what he cannot do – let it happen. Too much being in his head. Too much writing, too many words. He stands up and goes to the window, looking out into his garden. And then I realise that it's more complicated. He is jealous. It is not me who he wants, it is Bryony.

"So, what are you saying?" I ask.

He doesn't say anything at first, just stands there looking out of the window. But then he turns and looks at me directly.

"I am saying that you are to come back here, back to my house. I am not quite sure what I have planned for you, but you must come back here."

Something shifts. Something inside me shifts.

"I can't do that," I say.

"What do you mean, 'you can't do that'? Who do you think is writing this down? Whose story do you think this is?" he says.

"Not yours," I say.

William laughs. "That," he says, "is an illusion."

"If so, it is an illusion that you have created."

And then I stand up and walk out of his house. I go back to Bryony.

PART FIVE

ENDING AND BEGINNING

CHAPTER THIRTY-NINE

S omething shocking has happened. Yesterday morning Bryony received a text from William, asking her to go and see him. Urgently. So, she did. When she came back, I could see she had been crying. We sat down on the sofa, side by side, her head drooped and her hands held tight between her knees in the folds of her dress.

"What's happened?" I said.

"Something I wasn't expecting."

"But what is it?"

For a moment she looked at me as if she didn't want to tell me. Then she said, "William is sending me back to London."

"What do you mean?"

"Well, just that. He told me that Veronica has accepted an invitation to join the Orchestre de Paris as part of a six month exchange."

"Did you know this?"

"No, but William says it has only just been arranged. And then he told me that she is going to ask me what she should do with the house in Battersea, and that when she does, I am to tell her that I intend to return to London and live there, at least while she is away and perhaps longer. He hasn't decided."

"What do you mean, 'He hasn't decided'?"

"Just that. As he chooses. I have no choice. It's all been written down. I am to leave my house here and go back to London, to live once again in the house in Battersea. I do not understand why it has to happen."

I took her in my arms and held her. I was speechless. I had come to assume that Bryony would always be in Thorpeness and that our friendship would be there for ever. Now she was being taken away, taken back to London.

We talked a bit about what this meant for her and what was to happen to her house by the sea, and she said she didn't know, but that she wanted to keep it and come to it when she could. Neither of us really knew what to do or what to say. And for the first time in my life as Abraham Soar, I felt anger.

"I must go and speak to him."

"Yes, of course. It won't do any good, though."

"Can you drop me off?"

We drove to William's house. Bryony asked if I wanted her to come in with me, but I said no.

William was in his study and I walked in. He looked up.

"Hi Abraham, how are you today?"

"Not good."

"Oh, why is that?"

"I think you must know."

"Know what?"

"I think you must know that Bryony has told me she is leaving Thorpeness and going back to her house in London."

"Oh, yes that. Yes, of course. Sorry about that."

"Sorry? What do you mean, sorry?"

"Well, with Veronica going to Paris, I thought it was an opportunity for Bryony to go back to London and perhaps get to know her old friends again. You know, go to the theatre, maybe to the ballet. I thought it was time for her to come alive again."

"Come alive? You don't think she is 'alive' living by the sea?"

"Well, not really. It's been a bit of an escape for her. You know, part of her grieving."

"What do you know about grieving?"

"Not much, I suppose."

"No, not much. And what about me? Did you think about me, and how Bryony and I might feel about being separated like this?"

"Oh, come on Abraham. You know you're only a fiction. I hardly think you can really *feel* anything."

I couldn't believe he had said that.

"How dare you, William. Perhaps you're unable to feel much, unable to love and be loved, but I most certainly can. And I love Bryony. When she goes, I will too. I will not live here, with you."

"I think you'll live wherever I say," said William.

"Let's see," I said.

But it was no good and I felt impotent. Suddenly, all my energy had gone. I could not fight him. I walked out of his house, slowly back through the town and down the costal path, towards Sandy Bar. I was hardly aware of putting one foot in front of another. I couldn't go back to Bryony's house. Not straight away. And so, I walked down to the shore-line and sat on the shingle.

After a while, I heard someone walking towards me. Bryony. She took my arm and we sat there together without a word until we went back to the house, to our favourite spot on the veranda. Tabatha came and sat beside us.

"I told you it would make no difference," she said.

191

"I know."

I was shaking and Bryony took me in her arms and held me.

"I suppose," Bryony said, "this is the price we pay for being what we are, a fiction, part of someone else's world."

We sat there together, I don't know for how long, but neither of us could speak. At that moment, both of us were at a loss. Completely. After a while, Bryony stood up and walked into the kitchen.

"Tea?" she asked.

"Yes, that would be good."

We sat and drank our tea.

"When are you leaving?"

"Tomorrow. I have to take the nine fifty-seven train from Saxmundham."

"How will you get there?"

"William is taking me to the station, and I shall leave my car here, at least for the time being. I can put most of what I need into a couple of suitcases and leave the rest here. Everything else I need is already at the house in London. I've never moved it all here."

"Well, that's one good thing."

"Yes, I suppose so. What will you do?

"I don't know. William has said that I am to go back to his house."

"Well, just in case you need it, I'll give you a key to this house. I would like to think of you being here."

I smiled at her. I couldn't really believe we were having this conversation, but I took the key and put it in my pocket.

"I feel so helpless, I said. "Helpless and hopeless."

"Me too."

We shrank back onto William's page.

The next day, William arrived in his car to collect Bryony and put her on the train, asking me to be ready so that on his return he could pick me up and take me back to his house. I had already packed, but hadn't had breakfast. I waited. Empty.

When we arrived at William's house, I put my bag down in my bedroom and walked through to the kitchen to make some tea, taking the Ryvita and marmalade from the cupboard, mechanically going through a routine I had been through a hundred times. I made some breakfast, but it gave me no pleasure. It seemed futile. I had imagined Tabatha back with me, but she was not pleased. She sat upright on the back of the sofa and looked at me, her tail twitching.

"What's going on? Why am I back here? Where is Bryony?"

I told her what had happened and why we couldn't stay at Sandy Bar.

"I liked it there. I was settled in," she said. "I knew my way around. And now suddenly I'm back here. Thanks very much."

"It's not my fault," I said, although I realised that this did not seem an adequate explanation.

"Well, whose fault is it?"

"It's William's. It's William's story."

"And that's it, is it? It's William's story. That's it?"

"I'm afraid it is."

"For heaven's sake, Abraham. Pull yourself together and get a life."

And with that she walked away, tail held high.

CHAPTER FORTY

And so, the days have passed. The weeks. Christmas has come and gone and I have heard nothing from Bryony. I haven't been back to her house, I've stayed here, stayed where I have been put. William seems to have fallen into a kind of distraction. Sullen and hardly talking to me. I think he has lost interest in the story, the story about Bryony and me. It is as if he hasn't been able to think of anything else for us to do. We have been set aside, left behind. Well, I have anyway. A couple of days ago he went to stay with his friends in Norfolk. Didn't say anything, just went off in Zoe. So, here I am on my own. Abandoned. I have picked up my tapestry and begun to stitch. In from the back, up and over to the right and down. Red and yellow and green. It brings a certain peacefulness, I suppose. In and up and over to the right and down…

And then, whilst I am stitching, it comes to me. Of course! As my mind becomes still I know what to do. If William has forgotten about us, he needs to be reminded. He needs a nudge. Suddenly it is obvious. What is needed is a text. Why hadn't I thought about it before? Could it have been that I, too, have been part of William's forgetting? If so, perhaps I need to be part of his re-awakening. I walk through to my bedroom and pick up my iPhone. I have not been using it so it needs charging. I carry it through to William's study and plug it in. An hour later I have enough charge, and so, I begin.

Hi Bryony! It's me. How are you?

Swoosh!

Although I didn't know it at the time, at that moment, in a sitting room overlooking the marshes in Norfolk, William put down the book he was reading and thought about me. He took out his laptop and opened the file marked 'Abraham Soar'.

I have kept my phone close by, looking for the bubble, hoping that Bryony is there. But there is no bubble. I wait. In, up, over to the right, down. It's all I can do. Wait.

I wait for the whole day. Then in the evening, Ping! She's there.

Hi Abraham! How good to hear from you. Sorry I didn't reply before. I had my phone turned off. I had rather given up on it. But for some reason, I turned it on. And there you were. How are you?

There is a God!

I reply.

I wasn't sure it would work, and I guess until I did it, it wouldn't! I've been in a dark place. A deep nothing. I think William has lost interest in me.

Swoosh! Ping!

Me too. I think he has lost interest in me too. Having put me here, nothing else has happened. All that stuff about concerts and going to the theatre? Nothing! But perhaps you have woken him up?

Now I realise what is happening. William has started writing. There is another bubble. Bryony. Ping!

Call me.

Of course, I should call her! I stop texting and ring her mobile number. She answers at once. Her voice.

"It is so good to be able to talk to you again," she says. "Are you on your own? Can we talk?"

"Yes, just me. William has gone to visit friends in Norfolk. How wonderful to hear your voice. Why didn't we do this before? It's been weeks. We didn't even speak at Christmas."

"How is Tabatha?"

"Very disgruntled. In fact I haven't been able to find her for a while. I'm wondering whether she has gone back to Thorpeness. Perhaps she has decided to imagine her own world?"

"That's very odd indeed. Can a cat imagine her own world?"

"Why not? We thought we couldn't, didn't we, and then we found we could. I think Tabatha is every bit as smart as we are!"

"I think you're right."

We laugh. Oh, how good that feels.

"Have you been back to the house?"

"No."

"But do you think you could? I mean, now? Now that we've spoken. Do you think you could? I'd like to know that everything is okay at Sandy Bar. You have the key."

"If I go, will you come?"

"Yes. Why not?"

"Why not, indeed!"

And again we laugh.

We end our call and I go to my room and start packing. I call Squirrel Taxis and ask them to come and pick me up. I'll be ready in half an hour. I walk into William's study and leave him a note.

Bryony is coming back to her house and I have gone to stay with her.

I cannot quite believe it. I am alive.

CHAPTER FORTY-ONE

It is the morning at Sandy Bar. When I arrived at the house last night and opened the door, who do you think was sitting curled up on the sofa? Yes, of course it was Tabatha. She lifted her head as if she had been expecting me.

"How did you get here?" I said.

"Well, how do you think? I walked."

"But how did you get into the house?"

"Through the cat flap."

"But there isn't one."

"Oh, yes there is."

And when I turned to look, there it was in the kitchen door.

"How did that get there?"

"I imagined it."

"You imagined a cat flap?"

"Yes, of course. If you can imagine a cat, I can imagine a cat flap. Why not?"

Yes, of course, why not?

"Well, I'm very pleased to see you."

"Are you? After I'd gone, you didn't do much to find me."

"I didn't know where you were."

"But that's the whole point, Abraham. When someone has gone, not knowing where they are is where you have to start. That's where trying to find them starts from. Anyway, this is my sleeping time and I would like to be left alone."

With that, she placed her chin on her paws, closed her eyes and went back to sleep. I texted Bryony.

> I am here! And so is Tabatha. She walked here and then found her way into the house through an imaginary cat flap!

Immediately she replies.

> Send her my love and tell her she is very clever.

Now I am hungry. I shall have to shop. Not having any money is a problem, but after we spoke last night, Bryony rang the village store to tell them I would be coming in for provisions for her, and would they put them on her account. They agreed. Bryony's train will arrive at Saxmundham just before ten o'clock tomorrow morning. I have arranged a taxi to take me to the station to meet her.

CHAPTER FORTY-TWO

Bryony's train is due and I am waiting. There is a flashing of lights and a warning sound as the barrier swings down across the road. I look down the track and see the train. Just two rather old and dishevelled coaches. It stops and people begin to disembark. I am looking for her. At last, there she is at the far end of the platform with two large suitcases. I go to her and we hug, holding onto each other.

"How lovely to see you!"

"And to see you."

I take one of the cases and we wheel them behind us along the platform, cross over the rail track and put them in the taxi. We get in the back together. She takes my hand and smiles.

"How was the journey?"

"It was fine. The train to Ipswich was only half full and the same with the train to Saxmundham. Not a busy time of day."

We drive across the open fields with ditches running along the roadside, the road twisting and turning. And then we arrive. We pull up behind the house and between us manage to carry the cases to the back door and into the kitchen. We leave them there and walk through to the front of the house, opening the doors and the windows, and then we stand on the veranda and look out to sea.

"Home," says Bryony.

"Yes, welcome home my dear and lovely friend."

We walk back into the house. Tabatha is lying on the sofa. She jumps down and rubs her cheeks on Bryony's legs. Bryony reaches down to stroke her head and she pushes her nose into Bryony's hand. I wheel the cases into Bryony's bedroom. Bryony takes off her coat, throws it onto an armchair and flops down on to the sofa, smiling all the while.

"Tea?"

"Oh, yes please."

We sit, for the moment saying nothing, just taking in our being together again.

Then Bryony stands up and says, "Take me to the sea." And we walk across the shingle arm in arm, and down to the water's edge.

"Don't ever let me go away again," she says, and pulls herself close to me.

We walk back to the house and Bryony goes into her bedroom to begin her unpacking. It is good to hear her moving around the house. I have missed this. Just knowing she is there.

The sky is clear and the sun is bright. No wind. The murmuring of the waves.

I call out, "What shall we do for lunch?"

"Let's go and see Mel at the café."

"Excellent."

So we do, and Mel is pleased to see us.

"Where have you been?" she asks.

"Oh, just away," says Bryony. "We're back now."

"Oh, that's good," says Mel. "Perhaps we'll see a bit more of you?"

"You will," says Bryony.

And so, we have Mel's special cheese and vegetable pie with potatoes and Mel asks Bryony about being in London and we ask her what has been happening in Aldeburgh. Not much.

Tired by her journey and the early start of the day, Bryony has gone to her room for a rest. I have brought my tapestry with me from William's house. It helps my thoughts settle. To be back with Bryony, and for it to have happened so quickly – I can hardly believe it, but I suppose that is what fiction allows!

After about a couple of hours, Bryony is up and comes into the living room and sits beside me.

"That's coming on well," she says, taking the tapestry frame from me. "Can I have a go?"

"Of course." I thread a skein of red wool and show her where to start: secure the thread from the back by running it under stitches, then in, over, up to the right and down.

Bryony is thoughtful.

"It is so good to be here," she says. "And the miracle is that everything seems to be in place. Just as it was. Even Tabatha."

We laugh and Tabatha, who is curled on the sofa, twitches her ear, but remains asleep.

"I have begun to think about what coming back here means," says Bryony.

"And?"

"It must mean that William is at work again."

"Yes, I think it must."

"But something has changed. I think something has changed in him…I think he will want to talk to us."

"I suppose so, when he gets back."

"When I was resting, I texted him to say we were here."

"You did? What did he say?"

"He just said, 'Good'."

"Well, we'll see. In the meantime..."

"Yes, in the meantime…"

We let the thought linger.

Bryony reaches across and takes my arm, pulling me towards her. "And how have you been?"

"Well, a bit like you, I've been in a kind of nowhere. A lonely kind of nowhere."

"But now you're not. You're with me, and I have a feeling that something rather wonderful is about to begin."

"What do you mean?"

"I don't know, but it will be something unexpected."

Well, I hope I'm up to the adventure."

"My dear Abraham, your soul will rise on the wings of a seagull."

We laugh.

"That'll do."

CHAPTER FORTY-THREE

That night Bryony and I slept together. It had been such a long time, and we held each other close as if we might otherwise wake up and find it was a dream. As usual, Bryony went off to sleep easily, but I was restless, and still awake at midnight, I slipped out of bed, put on my dressing gown and came through to the living room. I wanted to hear the sea, so I opened the door to the veranda and walked out. The wind was up, but westerly, coming from behind the house. The tide was rising and the white topped waves turned and then thumped onto the sand and dragged the shingle back noisily. I had forgotten how comforting that sound had become. I closed the door, but could still hear the waves. There was a blanket on the armchair. I pulled it round me and lay on the sofa, following the rhythm of the sea. Soon, I was asleep.

It is six o'clock and I am awake and the dawn has already begun. I get out of bed and look out of the window. There is a bank of cloud on the horizon, but the rays of the sun are already edging it with gold. Soon, the sun rises and lays its pathway of light upon the water. Seagulls. I put on my coat and shoes and walk down to the water's edge. Nothing has changed. It is the same as it always has been. That is the mystery. That is the meaning.

I hear someone walking across the shingle and turn to see Bryony walking towards me, wrapping her coat around her, her arms folded across her chest. She has put on my woolly hat. I cannot help but laugh and she, knowing that I am laughing at her, laughs too. I hold open my arms and she comes to me and we embrace. A man walking his dog looks at us, but we care for nothing. We sit close together on the shingle to keep each other warm. We are as happy as we can be. It wasn't a dream.

"Shall we make breakfast?" says Bryony.

"Why not."

We walk back to the house and make tea and porridge and carry our cups and bowls and two blankets out onto the veranda, where we sit wrapped together.

Ping! A text on Bryony's phone. It is from William.

I'm back. Come and see me. Come this afternoon. Bring Abraham.

CHAPTER FORTY-FOUR

We park Bryony's car outside William's house. The gate is like a lychgate, with a tiled roof and oak posts. It is overgrown with ivy, roses and clematis. We open the stiff latch and walk up the garden path. William is watering some pots of pansies on the paved area by his front door. He turns and puts down the watering can. He has been waiting for us.

"Ah, there you are. Good to see you. What do you think of my pansies?"

There is a slight unease in his voice. Is he unsure of what is happening? I am.

We walk together into the house and William invites us to go through to the garden room while he makes tea.

"Do you want a hand?" says Bryony.

"Thank you," says William. "Could you take the plate of biscuits. I'll bring the tray."

Cups are poured and biscuits passed around. McVitie's Digestives, of course. Bryony and I are sitting on one of the large white sofas and William is on the other, at a right angle to us. For a while no one speaks. Then William puts down his cup, leans towards us and says, "I think I owe you an apology."

We are taken by surprise. We wait.

"I think I got lost, couldn't quite see the story. Actually, I think I panicked."

Again, we wait.

"You see, it's not all that straightforward, writing fiction. It's not straightforward at all. Well, that's what I find. It was okay to start with, but then I thought I had felt Abraham's need for company. I thought it was your need, Abraham, but now I see it was mine, too. And you were right. On the first page you were right. I wanted you to explore and experience feelings I was struggling with, and when I brought you along, Bryony, I surprised myself. Apart from being company for Abraham, you turned out to be…"

He hesitates, unsure whether or not to go on.

"You turned out to be just the sort of woman I should like to be with. I suppose it's not all that surprising."

Bryony smiles and William stops and drinks some of his tea.

"But then Abraham was falling in love with you, and you with him, and I felt a bit…I don't know, a bit excluded. I know it sounds stupid, but there we are."

So, it was as I had thought. William had become jealous, and when I look at Bryony I realise that she knows this, too.

"So, when you separated Abraham and me," she says, "you separated us, too: you and me, William. You separated us."

"But more than that," he says. "I separated myself from the possibility of love."

So, now he has begun to see it. Or part of it. Of course, I have known from the beginning that this story has all been about

William. His story, his quest. But now he sees it, too, and if this is true then it may be that my task is almost complete. I have brought him to the possibility of love.

Of course, this is only a beginning. You see, he is still caught in his own words, his own subtext. He thinks that it is Bryony that he has fallen in love with. He has fallen in love with the woman he put on the page. Why not? He created her as a woman to be loved, and now he thinks he loves her. So, now he wants to draw her away from me. I am no longer needed, or so he supposes. Could that happen? Is that what he is going to write? Will that be possible? Or has something else begun which he cannot know?

Later, when Bryony and I are back at Sandy Bar, I am sitting in the living room, reading, and Bryony is moving to and fro. I'm not sure what she is doing. We haven't talked much since we left William. I think we both need to take in what he has said. Although I know that William is not as much in charge as he thinks, the conversation with him has upset me. The possibility of loss. So, after we have had our supper, I tell Bryony that I am tired and want to be alone, and that I am going to have an early night and will sleep in the Guest House.

"See you in the morning," she says.

CHAPTER FORTY-FIVE

It is two o'clock in the morning. I am in bed having just woken up. *Vata* time. I get out of bed and then pull up the roller blind and open the window. Dark, the sky star-bright. The sea is almost silent. No wind.

I have almost forgotten how quiet the sea can be. At first, I hear nothing at all, but as my ears attune themselves to the silence I hear the faint sighing of the waves upon the shore. The tide is out, and one after the other, the waves turn onto the hard sand. Lights on the horizon, cargo ships, ferries, containers journeying into and out of Felixstowe. It is cold. I put on my dressing gown, go to the loo for an old man's pee, and then get back into bed. My hot-water bottle is still warm. Sleep. I sleep.

Six o'clock. Awake again. Another visit to the loo. I had left my window open. Now I look east, leaning on the window sill. I wait. The dawn comes, at first colouring the underside of a bank of low cloud. Pink. Seagulls crying. I go back to bed.

Twenty past six and the pink has spread low across the cloud above the sea. Dark, jagged clouds on the horizon. It is overcast.

Six thirty-five, I get up and again look out of the window. There is a light frost on the grass in front of the house and upon the sloping felt roof of the abandoned winch-hut on the shingle. A spring frost, a cold morning. Before the sun rises, the colour in the sky has begun to fade, spreading north. Low cloud. Within minutes the colour has almost gone. Just grey cloud and a layer of darker raincloud spreading low from the south-west.

Five to seven. Sunrise, but no sun. No colour apart from a faint patch of grey-pink in a rip, low in the clouds. Grey clouds above a grey sea and then the shingle bank. Now, for a moment, only for a moment, a smudge of pink on the underside of the clouds. Daybreak. An odd figure, a white haired man with a white beard and an empty shopping bag walks south towards Aldeburgh. An early riser.

One hour of my life – gone. Now a memory. Another memory. One day I shall say, "I remember that morning in Thorpeness when the dawn came up under a grey sky." It required so little of me. Just to bear witness. Another beginning, ancient and timeless. Beyond words.

And today it all begins.

CHAPTER FORTY-SIX

At breakfast Bryony leans across and takes my hand.
"Do you want to tell me about it?" she says.

"About what?"

"About what is troubling you."

I look at her and then I look away.

"Come on, tell me about it."

I take a deep breath. "It's about what William said yesterday."

"And?"

"What he said about you, and about his search for love."

Bryony laughs. "And you think that means William is falling in love with me. You do, don't you?"

"Well, yes I do."

"My darling, sweet Abraham, you have missed the point. William is not in love with me. How could he be? After all, he has created me in his imagination. I am a fiction. He is not in love with *me*, he is in love with what I represent. In fact, he is in love with what you *and* I represent."

"Which is?"

"Which is the capacity to love and be loved." She looks at me and smiles. "Get it?" she says.

"I think so. I thought that might be so, but somehow I couldn't be sure. Why are you sure when I am not?"

"I am obviously superior! Highly sensitive! Anyway, you and I have to go to Waitrose."

I suppose that William knows this, too, or at least he is beginning to understand it. The thing that Bryony and I have found so easy – falling in love – is the thing that he finds so difficult. So, as we drive back from Waitrose, I suggest that we invite him to come and visit us at Sandy Bar.

In that moment it comes to me. I turn to Bryony and say, "Perhaps we must love him?"

"Yes, I think we must."

And so, we invite William to come and visit us.

William is to come this morning. We chose a morning because it is the part of the day when the sun warms the veranda. He arrives, parks Zoe behind the house and then walks round to the front where we have put three chairs and a table on the veranda. Bryony and I are there, waiting for him.

"Come in, William," says Bryony. "Make yourself comfortable and I'll bring some tea. We've bought some of those biscuits you like."

William and I sit together on the veranda, and I ask him how he has been. He says he's been fine. Busy, of course. And then Bryony joins us with the tea-tray. We ask William about his trip to Norfolk and he says how much he enjoyed it, but that he is pleased to be home. And he tells us about some plans he has to go to a conference in Iceland; something about social change and transformation. But then the conversation eases and gradually we are taken by the stillness of the sea. That might sound like a strange thing to say because the sea is always moving with the swell and the ebb of the tide and with the wind as it moves across it. And yet, it feels still. This broad horizontal band of blue-grey, splashed with the light of the sun. Deeply still and timeless.

Bryony picks up her mug and holding it in both hands lets her gaze drift over the waves, towards the horizon. I do the same, following Bryony as she lets the sounds of the sea enclose her. Bryony and I are used to this, but for William it is clearly something he has not experienced before.

"It's odd, I live so near the sea, but hardly ever sit and look at it, or listen to it. When Abraham was living with me, we sometimes used to sit on the beach and look at the sea, but then my mind was always a scatter, always thinking about something else. And now, now that I am mostly on my own, I don't do it at all."

He stops, letting his gaze rest upon the horizon.

"Sitting with you here, I feel the quieting of my mind, and I can see why you love this place so much."

"It takes time," says Bryony, "but when you surrender yourself to it, when you let it be, you become so accustomed to it that after a while it is just the way you are. You no longer think about it. I suppose we are in love with it. *In* love, *with* it."

Feeling the stillness around him, William puts down his mug, stands up and goes to sit in front of us on the veranda step. Here we are, the three of us.

William turns to us.

"I'd like to talk to you more about this story I'm writing, the story about me and you. I have a feeling that we could write this story together, and that if we did, I might learn stuff that you both seem to know, even before I write it!"

"I think that would be good," says Bryony.

"Sitting here, I feel as if I am sitting at the edge of another world," he says.

I suppose he is.

CHAPTER FORTY-SEVEN

And so it was, that over the next few months, William became a regular visitor to the house by the sea. Sometimes he would just call by, but other times he would spend the morning or a whole day with us. We talked together, we walked together and we drank and ate together. At first, William thought that he would discover love by an endless discussion, turning over questions, looking for reasons and answers. But as the time went on, he began to see that this was not how it would be, and after a while, we would simply spend time together. Mostly, it was the walking that he liked. There was something about the rhythm of walking that helped him let go of his head. Saying nothing much, just walking by the sea or along the old railway line and through the reedbeds.

And then one weekend, after Veronica had returned from Paris, she came to stay and we asked if she would mind if we invited William to lunch. Just the four of us. Knowing what had happened before, when William had sent her mother back to London, she was a bit unsure of whether she wanted to meet him. But we told her what had happened since then, and I think she was intrigued. Anyway, she agreed to the lunch.

William arrived at midday, with a bottle of red wine. Veronica was in her attic room. We let her know that William was here and she came down and was introduced. Ignoring William's outstretched hand, she faced William with a cold and deliberate look in her eyes.

"So, you're William," she said, "the man who writes the stories. Our story."

William was taken aback. He must have known that Veronica was forthright, but now he could feel something else. Hostility.

"Well, yes I am, although recently that seems to have become less clear."

Veronica had more to say, and now there was anger in her voice. She was about to say something that she had thought about ever since he had taken her mother back to London; ever since he had hurt two people she loved.

"If you write about people, you should let them speak to you. Otherwise, how will you know who they are, rather than who you think they are? Or even, who you want them to be? I think it would be good for you to learn to listen."

William did not reply.

"And in the meantime, stay out of my life."

And with that she turned away from William, almost colliding with her mother, who was carrying a bowl of salad in one hand and tomato and cheese tart in the other.

William was clearly shocked and embarrassed by Veronica's outburst, and I could find nothing to say. I took the salad bowl from Bryony and put it in the centre of the table, whilst she put the tart in front of her and offered a slice to William.

"Shall we eat?" she said.

"Would you like a glass of wine?" I asked.

"Yes, that would be lovely," he said.

And so, the lunch began.

Veronica took her place at the table, watching William with some suspicion. He felt her distance. Bryony tried to lead the conversation by asking William what he was working on, but Veronica had made him nervous and he was hesitant. The lunch came to an end, and William said he had to get back; that he had some work he had to do.

After he had gone, Bryony was cross.

"Really, Veronica, did you have to make William feel so unwelcome?"

"But don't you see what he's doing?" she replied.

"What do you mean?"

"Well, he's using you. He is still using you. He may be talking about love, but it's his love, his need. It's all about what you can give to him. It's all about him taking something from you."

Her voice was now raised.

"For heaven's sake, Mum," she said, "where is your spine? Where are the boundaries? 'William this and William that.' What about you and Abraham? He may be the author of this book, but he is not the author of your life. And he is not a child!"

For a while none of us spoke. We cleared the table and put the plates and the cutlery into the dishwasher. Veronica was slumped on the sofa, Tabatha beside her, asleep, seemingly unaware of any disturbance. I brought the bottle of wine through and offered Veronica a glass. She accepted, and I poured one for Bryony and one for me. We sat looking at each other not knowing what to say. Then Veronica said she was sorry she had spoken to her mother like that, spoken angrily.

Bryony went to sit beside her, taking her hand. "No, but you're right," she said. "Of course you're right." It all began to fall away. The fiction, the control. It fell away.

In the afternoon, Veronica and I went for a walk along the beach. She was quiet, but she took my arm. We walked slowly until we came to an old and abandoned wooden fishing boat, left on the shingle bank to waste away, its paint fading, its prow pointing down towards a sea that would never again bear its weight. We sat down and leant against its side, sheltered from the northerly wind. It is sometimes uncomfortable for me, living as I do between worlds, the fictional world of Abraham and the world of my spirit being. But that afternoon I knew I was Abraham Soar who loved Bryony Sanders and was fond of her daughter Veronica, sitting here beside me, sorting through the shingle, selecting smooth round stones and ones that had a hole all the way through.

This young woman had set us free.

CHAPTER FORTY-EIGHT

A nd so, the change began. Over the next weeks, we continued our work with William, but now we did so not
as servants but as friends. Loving friends. For, despite being
shaped and sometimes hurt by him, we loved him too.

And something in me has shifted. It's as if I have become
more myself. I no longer worry about William and the story
he is writing, because I am becoming part of something else,
part of my own landscape. Especially the sea and the river.
I have started to study the tides and the phases of the moon,
and I have bought a notebook and am marking them down, so
that I become more attuned to them. We are today in the dark
phase of the moon cycle, three days when no moon appears
in the sky. The old moon has gone and the new moon has yet
to come. I set down the times of high water and low water,
moon rise and the quarters of the moon. New, waxing, full
and waning. The dark days make me think of Veronica, the
darkness of her hair and the way she withdraws. And as the
new moon waxes and becomes full I think of Bryony. I now
walk every day, setting off after breakfast. Sometimes I walk
alone and sometimes Bryony walks with me. And I with her.
With the coming of summer, the days are warmer. Sometimes

I come home by lunchtime and sometimes not until teatime, but that is the latest for me. I like to be home by evening.

The evening is a special time for being with Bryony. Do you remember I once told you how much I prefer dawn and dusk, especially dusk, with its a mixture of light and darkness, sitting on the veranda, watching the last of the light disappear? I like the journey towards darkness. Like Orpheus entering the underworld, but as he returned towards the light he could not resist looking back for Eurydice and she slipped away. I read that. I have started reading books about the moon, and the myths of the Ancient Greeks. I don't know why. Bryony buys them for me.

This morning I checked my moon calendar and the tide table. The moon is dark. The high tide in Aldeburgh Bay is 10.25 this morning and the high tide at the river will be 12.25, two hours later. A morning tide, not very high because the moon is resting. It will be low tide in the bay by teatime. All afternoon the tide will ebb and my energy will fall away, too. But this morning I will walk to the river to see the top of the tide, and watch it turn. Then I too will re-turn, walk home. I'll be home for a late lunch. I will take my bottle of water. Water to drink. Water inside, water outside. I seem to need the water, inside and out.

The ocean and the moon, these are my new loves. Aphrodite and Selene. I sit and listen to the sea call out and I watch the moon in its passage across the sky, east to west, before she disappears from view beneath the western horizon. And when she is at her brightest, sometimes I make sure I wake at night to be moonlit. I look at the moonlight lying on the sea.

Anyway, today there is no moon and I have walked to the river to watch the tide turn. I am standing on the riverbank.

After a while, irresistibly, the boats turn to the ebbing tide. At first, in the slack of high tide, some point this way and others that, caught by the wind or an eddy in the river, but then, as one, they turn, and face the tide, drawing back on their moorings. No sound, just a turning and the occasional cry of a gull. I leave the river and walk back along the sea wall. Then along Crag Path. And then, leaving the town behind me, I walk between the sea and the marshes, northwards to Sandy Bar. Before I go into the house, I go down to the water's edge, where the tide has yet to turn. But it will.

Like a devoted lover, I linger for just one more moment.

CHAPTER FORTY-NINE

B reakfast at Sandy Bar. The sky is grey, the clouds mounting from the south-west, and the wind is up. The sea is agitated. There will be rain before long. Tabatha is asleep on the sofa and Bryony has just brought through toast. I am already drinking my tea, but she sits at the table and puts her hand on my arm to ask me to wait. I put down my mug of tea and take hold of her hand across the table. A moment of silence. We close our eyes and feel the stillness come upon us. We are grateful for being here. Together. Our breathing slows and we find the edge of that other place. This is good. Ever since the lunch with William and Veronica, we have given ourselves to each other. No longer needing permission.

I suppose, dear reader, that my life beside the sea must sound very repetitive. Well, it is. But I've told you about that before. Repetition is part of what my life is about. But isn't your life like that, too? Your story unfolds, but don't you have things that happen every day or every week? Isn't your life filled with patterns? Isn't that what it's really like? But perhaps you don't want to come to a book to find it? Perhaps you would rather be taken to exotic worlds of fantasy and high emotion? I get that, but that's not me. And isn't there something in the detailed pattern of our lives that is worth recognising? Staying with our lives.

Bryony is going to see William this morning. She asked me to go with her, but I said no. I think William now needs to talk to Bryony, not me. Do you think my task was just to help him find his way to her? I do. Well, I've done it haven't I! And I think that maybe it has to be Bryony who helps him go beyond this story, to have the courage to reach out to a real woman, not a fiction. He can't just have our love. He has to find his own.

Veronica is coming to stay the weekend after next, and she has been in touch with William to say that she wants to speak to him, to have a proper conversation with him. He has agreed. I was thinking that it's odd that she feels so strongly about being shaped by someone else, and yet there she sits in the orchestra being conducted, most often by a man. Perhaps that is why the quartet is so important to her. They play together, with each other. I must ask her about that. I hope William will listen to her – she has so much she could tell him about loving and being loved.

I get up from the table and take my plate, my knife and my cup into the kitchen, putting them into the dishwasher. When I come back I see that Tabatha is stretching and then washing.

"Are you okay?" I ask.

She pauses for a moment.

"You are a strange man, Abraham," she says. "You bring me into this world of yours, but spend almost no time at all taking care of me, and now you ask if I am okay. Do you imagine that when you are away I fret until you return?"

"Well, I don't know."

"Think about it. I have no existence without you. When you are not here, neither am I."

"What about walking back to Bryony's house and coming in through the cat flap?"

"Come on Abraham, you know that was you. Even if it was only a fleeting thought. It was you, wasn't it?"

"I suppose so."

"Of course you do."

She stands up, stretches again and walks into the kitchen, through the cat flap and out onto the dune. I really don't know where she goes from there, so perhaps she doesn't.

CHAPTER FIFTY

Veronica arrived late on Friday evening and has settled in to the attic room. She is going to see William in the morning.

That night I am awake more than usual. The moon is nearly full and shines into the window of the Guest House. I have placed a chair by the window so that I can sit and watch it rising just after midnight, wrapped in my dressing gown, my room silent and still. Soon, in a day or two, it will be on its journey towards darkness, and I shall feel that easing of my energy that comes with the waning moon. I wonder if Veronica feels that?

Breakfast, and we are planning our day. Bryony wants to go to Halesworth and I have asked Veronica if she would stay with me.

"I have something I want to show you."

"Okay, but remember I want to see William."

"Yes, of course. Let's meet up afterwards, and then we can have lunch together and go for a walk. We need to be at the river by four o'clock."

"Okay, let's do that."

So, everyone goes their way and I am left for the morning, wondering how Veronica will get on with William. She returns at half past twelve. I have made lunch: soup and Mel's sourdough bread.

"How did it go?"

"Actually, it went better than I thought it would. I don't think William is deliberately unkind, I think he is just thoughtless; so taken up with himself that he isn't aware of others. Everything centres round him. When I pointed out that we have our own lives to be lived, he just said, 'Yes, of course'. And it was almost as if he was grateful to me for letting him know how we feel about things. He made a lot of notes!"

"That sounds like William. A lot of notes."

"Anyway, he asked if I would look at the passages he writes that include me. Of course, I said yes."

"Is this soup okay?"

"Yes, it's lovely."

We finish our lunch.

"So, where are you taking me?"

"To the river. I want to show you the turn of the tide."

"When shall we go?"

"In about an hour."

We walk along the shore-line and then up into the town, along the High Street and the unmade road between the sea wall and the water meadows, until we come to the river, taking the pathway of the river wall and then stopping. The tide is full and slack. There is no wind and the boats are still pointing into the tide. Now we have to wait and watch. We sit on the riverbank. Then it happens. One by one and together the boats begin to turn as the tide starts to ebb. First, in the slack water, there is no change, but then as the ebb takes hold, they turn to face the falling tide. It's a dance, a quadrille. Now the ebb is in full flow and a new order has begun. As the tide gains strength the boats pull against their moorings, as if they are eager to follow the ebb down-river.

"You see what the moon does? Aphrodite and Selene dance, turn and turn. One holding the other around her waist."

Veronica is still.

We wait a little longer and then, without speaking, we stand up and begin to walk home.

"Veronica, I want to ask you something."

"Yes?"

"Something about the darkness."

She takes my arm and smiles.

"No one ever asks me about that," she says.

"Well, I am."

"So, why are you asking?"

"I don't really know, except that I have seen you withdraw into something that feels like darkness. And you've told me about being sensitive to vibrations and changes of mood. Like the sea."

"Is that how you see me?" she says. "A dark woman?"

We laugh.

"Well, if I do, I find the dark comforting."

"Me, too. I always have. But I think I also need balance. Perhaps that is why I like coming to see Mum so much. She is brightness and light to my darkness."

"But what do you find in the darkness?"

We stop while she thinks about what I have asked her.

"I find sustenance," she says.

That's it. That is what I find, too. We have come to idolise the light, but it is in the darkness that we find renewal.

"I have a book I would like to share with you," she says. "Actually, I'll give it to you. It is the teachings of a Zen monk

231

given to a woman called Laurie. They call him 'his monkness', which I like. And there is one part where he talks about the peacefulness of the moonlight, starlight and the sound of the sea. He says, 'Go there, where your Beloved lives.' Isn't that how you feel about the sea? Isn't that how you feel about your Beloved?"

CHAPTER FIFTY-ONE

This happened. I am heartbroken and I am standing in the sea.

Last night Rufus and Dotty came to stay with Bryony, and this morning after breakfast they began to tell us about a report they had been reading about the pollution of the oceans.

"One million sea birds are killed by marine litter every year," said Rufus, "and the plastic is killing dolphins and whales and seals. Something like eighty per cent of marine debris is plastic, food wrappers, caps and lids, bottles and plastic bags. Much of it is cigarettes and filters. About one and a half billion pounds of trash enters the oceans every year, and there are five huge spiralling garbage patches in the oceans of the world. One of these, the Great Pacific Garbage Patch, is twice the size of Texas, seven million tons of garbage, up to nine feet deep. Some of it floats on the surface and some of it lies within the water or on the ocean floor. Four billion plastic microfibres per square kilometre litter the deep sea."

Suddenly, I couldn't bear it, couldn't take it in. I had stopped hearing what he was saying. All I could hear was the cry of seagulls and the thumping of waves upon the shore. I had to walk away. And then I remembered Sheila Brandon.

So, I came here. I walked across the shingle and stood at the water's edge. Now I can feel a great, great sadness welling up inside me and I have begun to cry. I have taken off my shoes and I am walking barefoot into the sea and the waves breaking on to the shore are all around me. Here I am. The water is cold, and my feet are cut and bruised by the stones on the sea bed. I walk further in. The easterly wind is in my face. It has lifted the sea into a tumult. I don't know what I am doing, but I want to say 'sorry' to my Beloved. I want Aphrodite to hear my confession and forgive me and my kind. But why should she?

Now I cannot stop crying, gasping, almost choking with a dreadful realisation of what we have done and what it must mean, the retribution that is to come.

"I am so ashamed. Forgive me. Forgive us."

"Abraham!"

I hear someone call my name. It's Rufus. I don't turn round, but take another step into the sea. I hear him running across the shingle.

"Abraham, what are you doing?"

Then I hear Bryony.

"Abraham! What are you doing?"

Now Rufus and Bryony are at the water's edge behind me. Again, it's Bryony's voice.

"For heaven's sake, Abraham!"

Yes, for heaven's sake.

I start to turn towards them and am almost knocked over by a wave. I stagger to keep my balance. Which way should I go? Further out or back to the shore? Another wave hits me. And then another. The tide is pulling me in.

For a moment nothing happens. But then I choose the shore. I walk out of the sea and reach out to Bryony who grabs my hand and pulls me to her. Rufus is holding my shoes.

When we get back to the house, Bryony strips my wet clothes off me and takes me into the bathroom, running a hot shower and helping me stand underneath it, the water of the shower running over my head and down my body. Although I am still shivering, the warmth of the water has restored me. Bryony wraps warm towels around me and rubs me until I am dry, then she gives me a dressing gown and puts me in her bed, covering me with her duvet. Dotty appears with hot tea sweetened with honey. I sit up and Bryony puts pillows behind me. I feel old and foolish. The shivering is easing, but Bryony has rung the doctor and not long after, two 'first responders' in green shirts and yellow vests are by my bedside checking my heart and my chest and taking my temperature.

"What happened to you?"

"I walked into the sea."

"Swimming?"

"No, apologising."

They look at each other.

"Well, you are lucky that your friends pulled you out and took care of you. Maybe you should apologise to them?"

"Yes. I have and I will do again. Am I okay?"

"Yes, you're okay. Nothing serious. Rest up today."

"I will. Thank you. Sorry."

Once they have gone, Bryony comes and sits beside me. I can tell she is relieved, but also angry. Angry at me.

"You and I need to have a serious talk," she says.

I take her hand.

"Do you think William was trying to drown me?" I ask.

She shakes her head. "On the contrary," she says. "I think you were trying to drown and William saved you."

I think she's right.

"But why would he do that?"

"You are part of him. Without you, something is missing."

"But one day…"

"Not yet. A little longer."

CHAPTER FIFTY-TWO

That was a month ago. And afterwards it took me some time to recover and to get back to my walking. For a while I could do no more than stay at the house and watch the sea, my Beloved, who seemed to have forgiven me and quite forgotten my madness. If I was mad…but I'm not sure of anything at the moment. You see, I have lost interest in William. Bryony says he is making progress and that he and Marianne are going to have supper together. He has booked a table at The Lighthouse. Apparently, he told Bryony he was looking forward to it, but was unsure what to do, and so Bryony talked to him again about love, showing him how it can be. This 'being in love'. Perhaps, this time, he won't be afraid. For surely he must see that loving and the caring for each other, and yearning too – it is necessary. Holy Longing. It is necessary. It is the story of the Cosmos. Sister tide and brother wind – loving companions.

But I no longer care about William, and he is no longer writing my story. He may be writing it down, but he has become a mere scribe. He records my life, but he is no longer the author of it. Thank you Veronica. From your own strong, dark place you saw the danger, the absurdity.

And the strangest thing has happened, something I had not thought was possible. You see, I didn't understand how much of my existence was for me to choose, but it turns out that it is much more than I had imagined. So, here's the thing: I have chosen to *become* Abraham Soar. To make him my dwelling place. I am leaving William. Tomorrow I will go and see him and tell him.

William is surprised to see me. After all, he hadn't written it down. But here I am, standing at his door.

"Come in. I wasn't expecting you."

Exactly.

We walk into his kitchen and he offers me tea, which I decline.

We go through to the garden room and sit down.

"So, what can I do for you, Abraham?"

"Nothing."

"Nothing? So, why are you here?"

So, I say it.

"I have come to say goodbye."

"What?"

"I've come to let you know I am leaving you, or rather that I have left you. I left you yesterday. Teatime, yesterday."

William looks at me in disbelief.

"What are you talking about? What's all this about teatime yesterday?"

"That's when I left you. Yesterday teatime."

William stands up. He's trying to understand what I have said. He frowns at me.

"I'm not sure that leaving me is possible," he says. "You are my character. I am your storyteller."

"Well, you were, but now you're not. I have begun to tell my own story."

"And who are you?"

"I am Abraham Soar. I have become Abraham Soar. Not your Abraham Soar, but mine."

He laughs at me.

"Well, you may laugh, William, but that is how it is." Then I remember. "Actually, William, there is something you can do for me. It's in return for something I have done for you."

"Which is?"

"Until now, or until very recently, I served you, and my gift was to bring you to the pathway of loving, a first glimpse of how to love and be loved. I think you're nearly there, or so Bryony says. So, that is what I have done for you. Well, Bryony and I have, I suppose. But now I want you to do something for me."

"Oh, really?"

"Yes, really. If I am the narrator of my own story, I want you to write it down for me, to add it to what you have already written. A final part of the book. Its title will be 'Becoming Myself'."

In that moment he saw that something had changed, and he knew he could do nothing about it. He just knew it. I had served his purpose and now he was going to have to serve mine.

A different story. A different ending. The truth is, in that moment, it intrigued him. He smiled.

PART SIX

BECOMING MYSELF

CHAPTER FIFTY-THREE

A nd so, dear reader, the final part of this story begins. Or rather, the old story comes to an end and another one begins. I don't know what will be said, but I know I cannot resist it. I am back at Bryony's house and she is making supper for us. Companionship. I cannot do this without her. Not anymore. Never could really. There is a sweetness to being with Bryony, something I cannot put into words. It's just there. And of course, she's a dancer, and so she brings lightness and dance, too. Which is good because sometimes I get too dark and stuck. Not that I mind the dark. It's as it should be. And anyway, it's not the dark that is the problem, but the fear of the dark. I have learnt to be content with it. I've stopped trying to change what must be. Who I must be. I've become part of the dance.

Now that I don't sleep so much, the shape of the days and the nights is changing. Spread more evenly. And I like to keep Tabatha close by all the time. Wherever I am now, I imagine her with me. She is with me during the day and sometimes when I walk, unless I go too far and then she goes back and waits. And when I sleep alone, as I do most often, she is with me at night. Once she has been out for her evening prowl, she comes back and settles down on my bed. Around midnight.

I asked her the other day what she felt about all of this, and she said that it suited her. Those were her words. "It suits me," she said. You know where you are with Tabatha. Anyway, I don't think I would be able to imagine anything else. It wouldn't work.

So, this evening she is here curled up on the sofa beside me. Asleep, or at least with her eyes closed.

"Would you like to light the candle on the table?" asks Bryony.

So, I take the box of matches from the bookshelf and light the candle. Then I tell her.

"I went to see William this morning."

"And how was he?"

"Well, he was fine. But then I told him I had left him."

"You told him what?"

I explain all that had been said, and how I am now the author of my life. I knew the question she would ask.

"And how do I fit in?"

"That is for you to choose, Bryony. You can remain in William's story or you can be part of mine. Or it could be ours. We could write our story together."

She looks at me. Then she smiles and says, "I would like that."

She opens her arms and takes me in. "My darling Abraham, how clever you are. And how brave, too. You have rescued us!"

"Well, it was Veronica really."

For a long time, we hold on to each other.

You see, this is how it works, or seems to work for me. Once you have let go of the world that someone is writing for you, your part, the part that is close by, becomes sharper and more intense. Small things that otherwise would not have been noticed come into focus. And at the same time there is no separation, no disconnection. The spoon by the marmalade jar and the spread of the sea cannot be separated. This is what Veronica told me that day we were on the beach. When she moves inwards, into that darkness of which she is part, the intensity of her energy increases. You might think it would be otherwise; that the darkness would hide things that would best be shown in the light, but that is not how it is. On the contrary. The dark brings forth the light. And that is how it is for me. Everything is now sharper, more intense. The delight of being with Bryony is sometimes overwhelming. And then comes the quietness of the evening at supper time. Or the constant murmur of the sea, turning.

And I must tell you about being in love with Bryony: being *in* love *with* Bryony. Do you see what that means? I suppose I came to Bryony because William needed to discover her for himself, but I am the beneficiary. He made a mistake, he thought it was all in his head, but it was not. We were not. Our being together was not. And now it catches me, or perhaps I should say it gathers me up, gathers me into its force, the force of the Cosmos.

Then there is this. I know I am not a young man and that my passions may be somewhat subdued, but it seems to me that it is a mistake to substitute sex for love, or rather to become obsessed with one small aspect of love and thereby exclude its greater part. That's what has happened hasn't it?

In this world, isn't that what has happened? Too much sex and not enough love? And then we miss the greater part. Loving. The practice of loving and being loved. The practice of the everyday, small, infinitely varied ways of love. Not that sex is not part of love, it is. Even for an old man like me. But it only points us towards something that is much greater, points us towards Love with a capital 'L'. The Great Love of the Cosmos. If we are not careful, if we do not pay attention, we miss the wonder of Love. Bryony and I love each other, and sometimes we are entangled in physical intimacy, holding each other, losing ourselves to each other, receiving and giving. But most of the time, our love is elsewhere, in the detail: the touch of her hand on my arm; the conversation of our eyes. In these moments we come together, unite, become open to receive, offer ourselves for the other. And in these moments we are complete and require nothing else.

Having never been married, well not as far as I know, I am wondering whether I might ask Bryony to marry me. I don't know, of course, but I think there might be something about being married that we cannot experience just living together as we do – on and off! Would we feel different? I wonder. I'll ask her.

CHAPTER FIFTY-FOUR

B ut I never did.

CHAPTER FIFTY-FIVE

That was all some months ago and by becoming Abraham Soar there has been gain and loss. The loss is that by leaving William and becoming Abraham I have had to accept age and mortality, and with that, of course, the fear of sickness and death. The suffering that the Buddha told us about. For that is the cost of leaving the ageless world of spirit and entering the human condition. But, dear reader, I have to tell you that the gain far outweighs the loss. For the gain of loving and being loved is without price. And, of course, I am blessed in having no past. Even becoming Abraham has not given me a memory of who I may have been. I suppose I'm a late starter! A blessing. If I had known my past, I have no doubt that there would have been all sorts of things I would have regretted. Things done and not done. Things said and not said. Even shame. Yes, there would have been some shame I am sure. But I have none of that. No overhanging grey clouds of misery and guilt. A clear sky, and my love for Bryony, which is ever-present.

And now I have to take responsibility for my own life, drawing strength from wherever I can, from whatever I can. As Veronica does from her dark place, and as Bryony does from her memories and her family. For me it comes from the place and landscape of my being. This morning we are sitting on the shingle, wrapped in coats and scarves and woolly hats, the sun lighting the world with a pale warmth. Bryony knows all that I know.

"When we sit here like this," she says, "there is nothing but you and me. It's as if we have become part of this landscape. This wonderful gift to us."

"And tea in a round mug, and marmalade on sourdough toast," I say.

"Those, too."

It's a kind of confession, a kind of surrender. And we sit side by side.

But it didn't work for William. He was not ready. Despite all that Bryony and I had shared with him, he couldn't overcome his fear. Supper with Marianne was just that. He remains alone, writing things down. He will have to find another way. I thought he came close: there were moments when he seemed to catch sight of what he was seeking. But then he lost it.

And when Bryony and I left him, it was a set-back. He knew he would have to start again, and perhaps he could not recover. Perhaps he never will.

CHAPTER FIFTY-SIX

Now that I have become myself, I have discovered something. It's about being at peace. I had thought that peacefulness would come from letting go, from some blissful state of detachment, but that is not how it is. Not for me. I have found peace, but I have found it not in detachment but in acceptance. In acceptance of the complex and often paradoxical state of being. Integration. It's about how we learn to bring each part of ourselves, each part of those we love and each part of our landscape, into the wholeness of our Being. Note the capital 'B'. It is a state of Grace. Born of Love.

In the meantime, I am Abraham Soar.

THE END...FOR NOW

37044993R00148

Printed in Poland
by Amazon Fulfillment
Poland Sp. z o.o., Wrocław